Praise for *Pride & Popularity*
by Jenni James

"This book was unputdownable. I highly recommend it to any fan of Jane Austen, young or old. Impatiently awaiting the rest of the series."

—Jenny Ellis, Jane Austen Society of North America

"*Pride & Popularity* is a delightful romantic comedy that will tug on the heartstrings of ladies—regardless of their age. . . . The fast-paced storyline will draw you in while the characters enchant you. . . . If you're looking for a refreshing reminder of how young, innocent love can break through even the most prideful of prejudices, you don't want to miss this one."

—Amanda Washington, author of *Chronicles of the Broken*

"This was an absolutely captivating read from the very first page. . . . I bought into every twist and turn and couldn't wait for Taylor and Chloe to actually get it together enough to become a couple."

—Shanti Krishnamurty, author of *Maid of Sherwood*

"One of the best remakes of *Pride and Prejudice* ever!"

—Jinx

"Loved this book. . . . Loved the heroine—she was fiesty and funny. . . . All in all, a very good read. "

—AJ Cole, author of *The Scarmap*

"This is so flippin' cute."

—Sweetly Southern

"Jenni James pulled me both into the story and into Chloe's hillarious predicaments, making me forget I've been out of high school for years. . . . Readers of all ages and circumstances will find themselves falling in love with Taylor, while laughing at Chloe's reactions to him."

—Andrea Pearson, author of *The Key of Kilenya*

"Dip into this excellent read and rediscover how relevant these 'Austen rewrites' are for a modern-day audience. The author has achieved that incredibly impressive and nigh-on-impossible feat—she's made one of the classic novels of our time entirely her own. Read and prepare to be swept away."

—Drew Cross, author of *BiteMARKS*

"Pride & Popularity is freaking A-MAZ-ING!"

—im-reading-here

"I love this book! I fell in love with Chloe right away! . . . This is a must-read."

—Tiffany

"I just absolutely love this story!! Eeep!! <3 <3 <3"

—Rachiee

"This was the best book I've ever read on [Wattpad]!!! So freaking good. And what was really cute is that it was sort of innocent and not like a trashy they-sleep-with-each-other-every-other-chapter kinda book."

—Christyfanning

"I couldn't stop reading. It's AMAZING!"

—just_smile22

The Jane Austen Diaries

Pride & Popularity
Northanger Alibi (Fall 2011)
Persuaded (Spring 2012)
Emmalee (Fall 2012)
Mansfield Ranch (Spring 2013)
Sensible & Sensational (Fall 2013)

The Jane Austen Diaries

PRIDE & POPULARITY

JENNI JAMES

Mary Ann

May you giggle & grin the whole way through!

Jenni James

This is a work of fiction, and the views expressed herein are the sole responsibility of the author. Likewise, characters, places, and incidents are either the product of the author's imagination or are represented fictitiously, and any resemblance to actual persons, living or dead, or actual events or locales, is entirely coincidental.

Inkberry Press, LLC
110 South 800 West
Brigham City, Utah 84302

Copyright © 2011 by Jenni James

ISBN: 978-0-9838293-0-0

To Judith A. Lansdowne, my favorite author.
Thank you, Judith, for all you are and all you've done.

ONE

♥

FIRST IMPRESSIONS

Summer before sophomore year

"Taylor Anderson is the hottest guy ever!" Madison said as she leaned in closer to me to catch a better view of him moving across the concrete basketball court in our local park.

To my right, Alyssa, who looked just like a younger Lucy Liu, practically burst an internal organ when she exclaimed, "I know. I've secretly dreamed of marrying him since I was ten." A pathetic sigh followed.

Disgusted with myself for somewhat agreeing with their drooling, I rolled my eyes. "Yeah, you and every other girl in this park. Look around you—is there a girl here *not* into Taylor?"

Alyssa flipped her long black hair and turned to stare at me with wide eyes. "Don't you like him? I thought everybody liked him."

Madison, still intent on Taylor, started to cheer as he made a basket. Her sporty, light brown ponytail bobbed up and down. Every other girl on the bleachers cheered and applauded, drowning out any answer I could've given Alyssa. Taylor pranced around with that silly grin on his face, waving to his adoring fan club, which only made them scream louder.

I rolled my eyes again. *Please, could this get any worse? The guy's got an ego the size of Madagascar. Let's just inflate it more, shall we?*

As if by some built in radar, fifteen-year-old Taylor's eyes honed in on me and my lack of enthusiasm. His lopsided grin worked all of its charm on the crowd as he approached our section of the bleachers. "Hey, Chloe," he hollered. "What's the deal? You weren't impressed?"

"Uh . . ." was all I could gasp as every female within a three-mile radius turned in my direction. I'm sure Taylor couldn't even hear me with all the noise.

"Come on! I bet I could get you to cheer for me. To prove it, this next basket's for you."

All the girls let out a collective sigh as he pointed his finger right at me. I could have cheerfully crawled under a rock and lived there for five years, mostly because of my body's reaction. *He knows my name. He called me Chloe. He knows my name!* my heart chanted as its speed tripled. Mesmerized by Taylor's retreating back, I watched slow-motion-movie-like as he rejoined the other players and laughed off their teasing remarks, which were muffled by the pounding in my ears.

"Chloe? Hello? Earth to Chloe." Madison's voice reached my subconscious.

"What? I'm here."

Alyssa giggled and nudged me with her elbow. "You were saying?"

I stared at her blankly. "Uh, saying?"

"You know, about *not* liking Taylor?"

A smirking Madison came to my rescue. "Come on, Alyssa. She's just a little shell-shocked, that's all. Honestly, who wouldn't be? Nobody can resist falling for him. It's a proven fact."

Smiling at my dazed expression, Madison nudged me again. "I would have to say the new girl's got it bad." Both of my neighbors and so-called friends burst into laughter.

Taylor must've heard them, because he paused and looked in our direction. Just as I was starting to breathe normally, he pointed right at me again and winked. In an instant, my face was as red as my very-berry lip gloss. Taylor noticed, and everyone noticed Taylor noticing me. He winked again and flashed those 100-watt pearly whites right at me. I was a goner. In the amount of time it takes a butterfly wing to beat, I was simpering and smiling back. Madison was right. No girl could resist the charm of Taylor Anderson, not even me.

With the knowledge of my defeat, Taylor turned just in time to catch the ball and *swoosh* it into the net. The fact that he had been standing on the three-point line made it a much louder "Taylor cheer" as the crowd of teenage girls rose to their feet. He beamed as he turned to me and mouthed, "That was for you."

"Get up!" Alyssa yelled, tugging on my arm.

"Come on!" Madison shouted as she literally pulled me to my feet. The other players were trying to congratulate Taylor, but he was still standing in the middle of the court, hands on his hips, daring me to cheer.

I gave up and let out a wild cheer to rival all the other girls on the bleachers, clapping my hands and jumping up and down. I couldn't help myself.

"Welcome to the Taylor Club, Chloe," Taylor said, moving to stand beneath me.

My heart flip-flopped as I stared down into his gorgeous blue eyes.

"I promise you won't regret it." With that he grinned, turned, and jogged to the other side of the court, where he sat next to one of the prettiest girls I had ever seen, then nonchalantly leaned over and kissed her. My heart and hands froze.

"Who is that?" I murmured.

Alyssa answered first. "That's Taylor's girlfriend."

"He has a girlfriend?" *He has a girlfriend!*

"Yeah. You didn't know?"

No, I didn't know! "I guess I never thought about it," I answered in a squeaky voice, but at least I didn't start to shake or anything.

Could I seriously have made a bigger fool of myself? How in the world did I, for two seconds, fall for his charm? Of course he has a girlfriend. She's probably the most popular girl in the whole school. The guy's obviously a player. I, of all people, should be able to withstand egotistical morons like Taylor Anderson.

My mind jolted back two months to Denver, Colorado, the assembly on the last day of school before summer break. I will never forget how Levi McFayden looked through the sea of people that separated us to find and connect with my eyes, or how he spoke so loudly that the whole school could hear him. He had pretended to still be talking to my friend Abbie, but everyone could see that the most popular boy at our school was looking straight at me.

"What? Why would I like Chloe Hart? What made you think I could ever like her? Just because I talk to someone doesn't mean I like them. Besides, she's a reject, plain and simple. I could never like a reject. So go run back to your friend and tell her my answer is no."

Levi had picked the last day of school to publicly humiliate me, and I was suddenly relieved my family was moving far away from Denver. I wanted to make a new start somewhere else—anywhere else. Yet here I found myself in a new place, getting ready to start at a new school, knowing the same awful thing could be repeated all over again.

Well, not this time. I'd learned my lesson. Popular guys like Taylor Anderson will never see girls for who they are, but I could see exactly what he was. *Taylor Anderson can officially remember this moment as the last time I will ever give him the time of day,* I thought. *What a self-centered, manipulative jerk.*

"Chloe, are you okay?" Alyssa asked.

"Y–yeah, I'm fine. I, uh, just remembered my mom needed me home by 3:00, so I'm gonna go, okay?"

Madison turned from the game. "You're heading home?"

"I need to." I smiled reassuringly. "Let me know how the game goes, all right?"

Both of my friends shared a girly look until Madison piped up. "Do you really need to ask? Isn't it obvious Taylor's team will win?"

"Is it?" I said.

"Hello? General rule of thumb, if you're going to be living in Farmington—Taylor's team always wins. He's the best at everything!"

"And don't forget, the cutest." Alyssa giggled.

My smile tightened. "Bye. I'll call you two later." I heard their combined chorus of "Okay, bye" as I walked down the steps of the bleachers. At the edge of the court, I came across two girls whispering.

"He's so hot! I mean honestly, can you believe there is anyone as hot as Taylor on this planet? Dark hair, blue eyes . . . like, *everyone* is in love with him."

Disgusted, I pushed my red curls off my face and then stomped away. *Not this girl! There is one thing I can safely promise myself. I will never fall in love with Taylor Anderson.*

TWO

♥

SURPRISE, SURPRISE!

Three years later: first day of school, senior year

"Chloe!"

As I spun around in the crowded hallway by my locker, Madison caught me up in a bear hug. She had gone to stay with her cousins in Florida for two months of summer break, and she had come back tan and beautiful. I laughed as I removed a piece of her streaked blond hair that was caught on my backpack.

"Wow! Maddi, you look gorgeous. You obviously had a great time in Florida."

Madison sighed. "It was wonderful!"

"So, tell me, did you find some amazingly hot lifeguard to sweep you off your feet?"

She rolled her eyes. "I wish." Then she glanced at me suspiciously. "So how about you? Did you find anyone this summer?"

I laughed. "Yeah, right. I just hung out and did my theater gig. Besides, every guy I'm remotely interested in ends up too self-centered and a total jerk anyway, so—"

15

"You know, Chloe, one of these days some guy is going to prove you wrong. And when he does you're going to fall for him hard. Personally, I can't wait."

"Whatever." I laughed and shook my head. Madison was crazy, of course, but something about the way she looked at me with one eyebrow raised made me uneasy. I decided it was a good time to change the subject. "Well, we may not have been so lucky, but wait till you hear about this Zack guy Alyssa's been talking about."

"Alyssa found a guy?"

"She hasn't told me much, but from what I can tell she's head over heels. I'm going to art class with her next, so I'll get the scoop for you."

"You have art next? Me too."

"Seriously?" I said, and she handed over her schedule to confirm. "No way!" We jumped up and down like a couple of eighth graders. The three of us had tried since we were freshmen to get a class together, but it never worked out.

"Chloe, wait up!"

At the sound of Alyssa's voice, Maddi and I both turned to see her running through the crowded hall. Her cello case bounced up and down on her back as she headed straight for us. She halted midway. "Madison? Madison! It's you. Eeeh! You look so good. I love your hair."

Excitedly, we joined her and took a few seconds to stare at each other before we all said at the same time, "Group hug?" We stood there hugging each other, taking up most of the hallway. Later, we would have time to catch up with all of our other friends, but right now it was just us. This year was going to be good—I just knew it.

I glanced at my watch. "Hey, we've got to hurry if we're going to beat the bell. I hope there's a table left for all of us."

We rushed into the art room just as the bell rang, giggling while the whole class witnessed our excellent example of how *not* to enter a classroom. With a glance at Ms. Bailey, our art teacher, I could see we were forgiven—barely. Hiding a grin, she raised an eyebrow and pointed to an empty table with four plastic blue chairs in the back of the room.

A whole table just for us. Yes. "Thank you, Ms. Bailey," I said as we almost skipped to the table.

"Yes. Well, girls, hurry and get situated while I call roll." Ms. Bailey scooped up a clipboard with a pen dangling from it and began to call out the names on her list. "Daniel Addison?"

At our table, we chattered and chuckled over our amazing good fortune. The energy in the room positively sizzled with excitement and anticipation. Then Ms. Bailey called out, "Taylor Anderson?"

It was like the summer when I was fourteen, all over again. My heart stopped, and I could feel myself begin to shrink to the size of a pea.

Taylor is here? He's in this class? With us? No! This was supposed to be our perfect year.

As I scanned the room, I saw excitement on almost every face. Clearly, our classmates were thrilled at the thought of the most popular guy in school gracing us with his presence every day. But there was no Taylor.

He isn't here. Taylor isn't here. Ha ha, I thought.

"Taylor? Taylor Anderson, are you present?" asked a worried Ms. Bailey.

He had probably changed his schedule at the last minute, I decided. I was prepared to shout with glee when a pretty blond sophomore raised her hand at the table next to us.

"Ms. Bailey, I was told Taylor was in California saying goodbye to his girlfriend, who's going to college. He's supposed to be here Thursday."

"Thank you, Miss—"

The blond girl blushed. "Oh, I'm Emma . . . Emmalee Bradford. My name is probably next on your list. My stepbrother Zack Bradford, who is a senior this year, is, like, Taylor's best friend."

Alyssa gasped. "That's Zack's sister?"

I thought she was going to have a heart attack. "His stepsister. So? What of it? Oh! *He's* the Zack you're going out with?"

"I'm not going out with him. I just kind of like him. Well, a lot." Alyssa grinned shyly.

"We are definitely hitting Colleen's Diner after school," Madison announced. Then she zeroed in on Alyssa. "Zack Bradford? Sheez. I want to know everything."

"Chloe Hart is—present."

I looked up as Ms. Bailey marked my name on her clipboard. Good ol' Ms. Bailey. She had been my art teacher all throughout high school. I loved this class. Freedom to draw and design and create was something that moved me toward art more than anything. Yeah, so we had to do the assignments she gave us—portraits, still life, watercolor, or whatever—yet she always let us express ourselves however we wanted. If I wanted to paint my lion purple with a green mustache and an orange Gucci bag, I could. Not that I ever had. It was the fact that it was up to me how I painted the subject that made Ms. Bailey so cool. She was a teacher first, but a friend always.

Why oh why is Taylor Anderson in here, of all places? He's going to mess up everything.

I knew he liked art. Everybody knew Taylor liked art. But with eight art periods to choose from, I never thought we would be in the same class together.

I have seriously got to get a grip. There is absolutely no reason for Taylor to have this sort of effect on me. So he is the most annoying, arrogant, pig-headed idiot—that doesn't mean he's going to concern me in any way. Ms. B. may not be able to get the rest of the class to work since they'll all be staring at him, but I am way above that. I am smarter than every other girl in this room. I see him for who he is. He doesn't fool me with his carefree mask and witty charm, and he never will. There. That sounded good. But why did he have to be so, so good-looking?

{♥}

"Okay, fess up. I want to hear all about Zack and how you and he—you know, met," Madison said as we waited for our milkshakes at Colleen's Diner.

Alyssa fidgeted and made that funny, squeaky noise that happens when you squirm on vinyl-covered booths. "He, well, he . . . he likes the cello."

"Okay, and? How did you meet him? What were you doing? How did he know you played the cello? Did he see you perform or something? Come on, Alyssa, I'm dying for some exciting news already, so tell me!" Madison begged.

"All right, but you have to promise not to laugh, okay?" She turned to me. "Okay?"

We both nodded.

As if I would. Well, maybe a little.

"You know how my family and I go to the rest home in Bloomfield every Sunday evening so I can play for my grandpa, right? Actually, I'm pretty popular, and now I perform in their main lounge area so anyone who wants to can come in and listen. Some nights I even get requests. It's like a standing gig every Sunday night at 6:30." She winked at us.

"Really? I had no idea," I said. "You should invite us sometime."

"Yeah, we could be in the front row and hold up signs that say, 'Alyssa rocks, so get your rocker and rock along with her!'" Madison added.

We all burst into giggles, but Madison quickly got back on track. "Okay, so about Zack?"

"Well, what you may not know, and what I definitely didn't know," said Alyssa, "was that Zack goes to the same rest home every Sunday afternoon to visit his grandma. Anyway, his grandma had told him about my playing. Which was cool, because his mom used to . . . Oh my gosh! Did you know his mom died of breast cancer?"

"What?" I almost dropped my drink.

Alyssa continued, "I mean I knew he had a stepmom and all, but I just always assumed his parents were divorced."

I was shocked. "So did I."

"So did I," Madison exclaimed. "Well, at least he's popular, you know?"

"Kind of a pathetic consolation prize for losing your mother," I said.

Madison nodded quietly for a moment before snapping back into interrogation mode. "Enough doom and gloom. Tell us what happened. You were about to say something else about his mom?"

"Oh, did you know his mom used to play the cello? Can you believe it? The cello. It's like fate or something."

"Now, that is cool," I said.

"That's not even the best part!" Alyssa leaned forward. "Zack's mom must've been an incredible player, because right before she died, when he was like seven or eight, she performed in a breast cancer fundraising event where her cello solo raised over $33,000! That's thirty-three *thousand* dollars! Can you believe it? The most I have ever raised for charity was $23.59.

No wait. It was $23.58. My punk little brother took his penny back after hearing me play."

Too funny. I love little Tanner. He's such a hoot. I tried not to smile.

Madison smothered a grin too. "Stop stalling already, Alyssa. Get to the good stuff."

"So there I was playing. This time, I guess Zack decided to stay and listen. I didn't even know he was there. You know how I get into my own zone when I'm performing? Anyway, later, he said that seeing me up there reminded him of his mom. And I won't go into how much of a compliment that was to me, because then Madison will get all testy again. So, before I knew it" —Alyssa went on, drowning out Maddi's protests— "my little recital was over and I was bowing, because they always make me bow when they clap. I tell you, old people can be pretty demanding." She looked to Madison. "Okay. I'm moving on.

"And as I bowed and bowed—they were especially moved that day, standing up and everything—I was starting to get embarrassed by all the attention. So, to stop my adoring fans, I did an extra dramatic swooshing curtsy thing. That should never be done in public and never will be done in public again, because as I was standing, my arm went way out and totally hit a stunned Zack right in the face! He was coming up to compliment me. The smack surprised him so much he lost his balance and fell backwards. He knocked over a whole cluster of fake trees, spilling rocks, foam, and fake moss everywhere. It was so humiliating."

"What? Oh my gosh. You knocked over Zack Bradford? That's how you met?" I couldn't help but laugh.

Madison laughed too. "This is hilarious! What did you do? What did he do?"

"Hey, you promised not to laugh." Alyssa leaned back. "Well, I was mortified, as you can imagine, and I think he was too. His face was all red, and he couldn't even look at me for a while. But it was okay, because we were both so busy. We helped the workers clean up the mess. It was after we collected the moss stuff, vacuumed the floor, and redecorated, that we were finally able to really talk to each other."

"So what did you say?" I asked.

Alyssa blushed. "Well, I told him he still had some moss in his hair. After laughing about it and getting what he could without a mirror, he let me remove the rest. It was as I was pulling the bits of pieces off the back of his head that he told me about his mom and why he wanted to come up and talk to me."

"Wow, Alyssa," I whispered. Madison was as still as I was.

"Yeah, it was a really nice moment for both of us," Alyssa went on. "Then I told him how my grandma and grandpa migrated here from China with just their instruments and a few dollars, and how it was because of them and their love of music that I play now. After that, Zack and I just sat on the couches and talked. It was really cool getting to see him as a normal guy."

I smiled. "Alyssa, he's one of the most popular guys in our school. I can't believe that was the Zack you've been talking about all the time."

"I was afraid you'd be mad at me if you knew he was Taylor's friend," she said.

"What, why? No, I'm happy for you, really!"

Madison smirked. "Well, we've *all* heard your thoughts on Taylor. It's no wonder she hesitated to bring up Zack." She turned to Alyssa. "He sounds like a great guy, and I think you should go for him."

"Go for him? I thought you were already going out with him," I said. "At least that's what it seemed like."

"No, not really. We just hang out at the rest home on Sundays. Usually, we'll play a mad game of Dominoes or Pinochle with our grandparents."

"Pinochle? It's gotta be love if you're playing Pinochle together," Madison teased.

"We're just friends," Alyssa said defensively. "Honest. Apart from quickly saying hi to me in the halls a couple of times, Zack never even spoke to me today, and we have two classes together."

What is it with popular guys shutting out people in front of their friends? I thought. *It's what makes me so mad about the "in" crowd. Everyone is so superficial. I hate to even think it, but Zack has an awesome chance at having a real, compassionate girlfriend for probably the first time in his life, and yet he's too scared to do anything about it. Guys like that are so fake. Of course, then there's Taylor Anderson, who's on a whole other level of shallow.*

At least I had three days to prepare to keep my equilibrium from tipping and making me dizzy whenever he was around. If Zack's example wasn't enough of an inducement to keep my head afloat—and keep me from drowning in the same silliness as the other girls around me—then I didn't know what was.

This seemed like an awesome little pep talk to give myself at the time. But I hadn't counted on one thing: Taylor showing up earlier than anyone could have predicted.

THREE

♥

PRIDE GOES BEFORE THE FALL

What guy comes home from a cross-country trip in the morning and attends school that day? Couldn't he have waited one more day instead of waltzing into art class with a little yellow slip from the office? Of course, he would pick *this* class to show up to.

You could literally feel the room spark to life. One by one, students became aware of the "Great" Taylor Anderson's presence. Collectively, clothes, hair, and work stations became tidy. I decided to leave mine a mess. That was until I looked down and noticed a large smear of green chalk down my arm and on the sleeve of my new white shirt. Frustrated, I stood up and headed for the sink. I was determined to not even glance Taylor's way. *This is perfect. He can sit somewhere, and I can pretend I never even knew he was here.*

"Chloe," Taylor exclaimed.

I panicked and began walking faster to the sink.

"It's nice to see the president of my fan club is finally in one of my classes."

I could feel each and every eye as they stared at my back while I turned the faucet on and began to scrub. *Why did I think ignoring him would work? Could the guy be any more conceited?*

He must've realized he wouldn't get a response from me, because the next thing I heard was, "Ms. Bailey, is that an empty chair at Chloe's table?"

What? He wouldn't dare! I jerked around and glared right at him. Too late. It was obvious from his grin that I had just given him the attention he'd been waiting for.

"I can sit there? Great, Ms. B. You're the best!"

Is Ms. B. blushing? Is there not a female on the planet able to resist this guy?

Out of the corner of my eye, I saw Taylor saunter over to our table. Whispered words of admiration came from Alyssa and Madison. *The traitors.* In disgust, I tried to drown them out as I turned the water on full blast. It worked, except that after five minutes of unnecessary scrubbing and loads of excess spray from the tap, not only was my sleeve soaking wet, but the whole bottom half of my shirt, too.

"Come on, Chloe, stop hiding," Taylor said. "Come over here and welcome me properly."

Does he have to say everything so loudly? Furious, I grabbed some paper towels and headed back to the table.

"I'm not hiding. I'm cleaning my shirt, thank you." Still not able to meet his eyes, I wiped my shirt as I walked. A couple of seconds later I wished I had looked up, because I literally tripped on a chair two feet from our table. *Nothing like falling at his feet in a heap.*

Taylor chuckled as he gently helped me up. "Whoa, copper top, you've gotta watch where you're going."

"Thanks," I muttered, brushing my curls out of the way. Just then, I realized the rest of the room was laughing at me. Of course, I had nobody to blame except myself and my silly pride, so I joined the others and laughed too.

I noticed Taylor breathed a sigh of relief when he saw my giggles. *Careful, Chloe, you might start thinking he actually cares.*

He surprised me further by making sure I sat down safely in my chair. Then he began to clean up the strewn paper towels I had dropped when I fell.

"You don't have to do that, Taylor. I'll clean it up." I started to rise.

"What, and not have the satisfaction of seeing me on my knees in front of you?"

I knew he said it only to stun me into sitting back down. It worked, more than he realized. *Remember, you can't stand him. Act like you would to anyone else.*

"Chloe, are you okay?"

I glanced over and found myself staring at Madison and Alyssa, who grinned back at me. I'd forgotten they were there! How could I forget my two best friends were right in front me?

"Uh, yeah. I'm fine, I think." I smiled back.

We couldn't say more because Taylor walked up right then and sat on the chair next to me, smiling in an arrogant and slightly magnetic way.

"So, girls, it looks like we're all here together. This is going to be an interesting year." He turned to me and asked, "Don't you think?"

I was so grateful the bell rang and saved me from having to answer him. Instantly, our table was crowded with art students vying for Taylor's attention. It was the perfect opportunity to escape. As quickly as possible I cleaned up my spot, grabbed my backpack, and headed out the door, leaving Alyssa and

Madison to fend for themselves. I'd apologize when I saw them later.

As I jogged down the crowded hallway, I nearly collided with Ethan, one of the greatest guys on the planet.

"Hey, girl! Where's the fire?" He hung his arm around my shoulders and started to walk with me to Advanced Placement English.

"Back there," I said. "I was trying to get as far away from it as possible."

"Gonna scorch you bad?"

You have no idea.

"Oh, hey." He shifted his backpack. "You still on for tonight? There's a big group of us headin' up to the Staircase for the opening night of the new season. They've all been saying how they're gonna beat my Jeep this time. You better be there. You're my good-luck charm." He playfully squeezed my shoulder.

"Um, four-wheeling or studying? Gee, that's a tough one. Of course I'll be there. Aren't I always there on Wednesdays?"

"Ever since you started coming it's been so much wilder," Ethan said. "I never knew a screaming, terrified girl would add that much excitement."

"I'm not scared. It's more like a roller coaster than anything."

It was the truth, too. Ethan's dad was not only a driving instructor, but also a professional four-wheel driver. He had taught Ethan and his brother Carson everything they knew. When you watched them, it was obvious they were good. Ethan and Carson hadn't even been allowed to start four-wheeling until they'd passed their dad's twelve-month course. My parents were a little apprehensive when the guys first asked me to join them on Wednesdays about a year ago. But after they met the brothers, Mom and Dad agreed to let me go as long as I only rode with Ethan or Carson. I became addicted to the exhilarating experience and had been going ever since.

"Chloe!" someone shouted from behind us.

I stopped just as we were entering the classroom and turned to see Taylor as he tried to catch up.

What is he doing? I wondered, my heart speeding up.

"Oh, so now you've got Anderson following you?" Ethan asked. "I'll save you a seat inside."

Just like that, he left. And then Taylor was right next to me—towering over me, actually. *When did he get so tall?* He stared at me for a few of seconds and then grinned. *He's not even winded. It's so not fair.* People had to squeeze to get past us into the classroom, and I realized we had begun to create a scene. I wondered what Taylor wanted, but I refused to be the first person to speak.

Finally, I couldn't stand it anymore and caved. "What do you want, Taylor?"

"You." His eyes captured mine.

Breathe, Chloe. Calm down.

"Me, to do what?" *That sounded good, surprisingly good.*

"To admit you missed me the past few days."

Hello? Is anybody here but me remembering you have a girlfriend? "You were gone? Huh, I never noticed. Well, guess I'll see you tomorrow. Bye, Taylor." I was still speaking as I turned and walked through the classroom door.

"Wahoo! I can't believe you had the guts to say that," Madison said as we rode home from school in her car.

"I can't believe he followed you to your English class," Alyssa added.

Jenni James

"I know. It's not like him. I can't figure what he's about." I shrugged. "I mean, the guy has a girlfriend, right?"

"It just seems weird. I wonder if he was coming to tell you something else and chickened out," Alyssa said. "Besides, there must've been a reason he was totally singling you out in the art room. I think he needs to ask you something but doesn't know how."

"What does he have to be scared of?" I wondered out loud. "No, I think he's just being a player. He saw an opportunity to make me uneasy and went for it. Of course, this time I stood my ground."

"Yeah, too bad you didn't stand your ground in art." Madison laughed, and Alyssa joined in.

"Hey, now, no fair. I was wiping my shirt." I giggled. "It *was* funny. Embarrassing, but so funny."

"Aren't you sorry you laughed at my episode with Zack now?"

"Yes," I answered Alyssa as she pulled up next to my house. "Well, it's Wednesday, so I won't be home tonight. I'll see you girls in the morning, okay? Thanks for the lift."

"Bye!" they said at the same time.

I shut the door and ran up the steps of my house. I turned to wave as the girls drove home, which was really only five or six houses down on the left side of the street. Alyssa and Madison lived right next door to each other. On the other side of the road was a huge neighborhood park. The chance to live across the street from the park was one of the reasons my parents bought our house.

"Hi, Mom," I called out as I dropped my backpack on the dining room table.

"Chloe? Is that you?" she called from the back of the house.

"Yep. Where are you?" I followed the smells and wandered into the kitchen, where I saw loads of cookies on cooling racks on the counter. Shortbread cookies, my favorite. "Hey, can I have a cookie?" I hollered.

"Sure," she answered.

Yes! I grabbed three extra-big ones.

"But only one. They're for my meeting tonight."

Aw, darn. Reluctantly, I put the two smallest cookies back. As I munched, I went in search of my mom.

"Here you are." I found her in my fifteen-year-old sister's room, holding a big, black trash bag. I watched, dumbfounded, as Mom tossed anything and everything she could find into it.

"What are you doing?" I gasped. There went Cassidy's favorite CD and iPod.

"I've told Cassidy over and over to clean her room or I was going to clean it for her." She groaned as she bent over to chuck my sister's winning soccer cleat into the bag. "For three weeks I've been patient." In went the other cleat. "So I figure now is the time to teach that girl a lesson."

Wow. Cassidy is gonna be mad. I stifled a giggle. "So what are you going to do with the bag?"

"Put it out by the trash bins and tell her I've thrown it away."

Holy cow! "You're serious?" *I wonder what my room looks like. I hope it's clean.*

"Yeah, I'm serious," Mom said, pushing back her blond curls as she stood up. "This room is disgusting, and she's going to start taking care of it or suffer the consequences."

I'm pretty sure my room was clean when I left this morning. Maybe a towel on the bed or something? Mental note: Check room ASAP and remove backpack from table. Mom's gone batty again.

I'd have to be blind to not see how determined my mom
was on this, so I let it go and changed the subject. No reason to
get her upset at me, too.

"Well, today's Wednesday, so I'll be out four-wheeling
later," I reminded her. Then, deciding to stay on her good side, I
asked, "Do you need me to do anything before I go?"

"You mean other than your homework and chores?" Mom
grinned as she tossed Cassidy's curling iron in the bag.

"Uh, yeah." I wondered how much all Cassidy's stuff was
worth.

"I am not really going to throw this stuff away. I'm just putting
it out by the trash to make her see how serious I am. So stop looking
at me like that." In went Cassidy's favorite shirt and jeans.

Well, that's a relief.

"Actually, there is something you can do for me. I need
you to go and pick your sister up from her ballet class in about
fifteen minutes, so I can finish this up."

"Oh, okay." *If I started now I could get farther into that
book I was reading for English.* "I'm gonna do some homework
before I head out." I turned to leave.

"I almost forgot. There was a call for you right before you
came home."

"A call?" I turned back. "Who from?"

"I don't know. It was one of your friends. I think he said—"
He? It was a he?

"You guys were in the same club or something. His name
was like Tyler or Tanner or—"

"Taylor," I interrupted. "Did he say what he wanted?" *What
is with this guy?*

"No. He did ask for you to call him back, though. His cell
number is on the kitchen counter by the phone. He sounded like
it was kind of urgent."

"Oh, it's probably just a question about something in art class today." I shrugged. "Thanks." I made my escape.

He hasn't even been home a full day, and already he has caused so much havoc to my well-being that I don't think I'm going to be able to last an entire year. It's ridiculous.

I wandered into the kitchen and glanced at Taylor Anderson's phone number. *This is Taylor's number. I have his personal phone number. How many girls would kill to have this number?* Briefly I thought of selling it on eBay or something. *I bet I'd make a mint. Ugh. How much weirder can this day get?*

Reaching over, I plucked the cordless phone out of the charger and started to press the buttons with trembling fingers.

Why does he want me to call? Does he really have something important to ask like Alyssa thinks, or is he just trying to unnerve me again? You know what, I can't handle this. Before I could push the last digit, I hung up the phone. If he wanted to talk to me that bad, he could call again.

I collected my backpack and crammed the offending number in my pocket. Then walked in my room and attempted to breathe normally again. Looking at my watch, I saw I only had twelve minutes left. So I picked up the assigned book, crashed on my bed, and tried to lose myself and my crazy thoughts in Jane Austen's *Sense and Sensibility.*

FOUR

YOU RANG?

Five minutes into the book, I still couldn't concentrate. I knew it had nothing to do with Miss Austen's writing ability and everything to do with a certain "urgent" phone call I needed to make. I pulled Taylor's phone number from my pocket and stared at it.

"Ugh. Please go away, Taylor Anderson," I said out loud. "I don't know why you find it so hilarious to pick on me, but do me a huge favor and leave me alone. Seriously, you can have any girl you want. Why drive me nuts? It makes no sense."

Great, Chloe. Just awesome. You're having a conversation with a crumbled piece of paper, which won't answer back no matter how long you stare at it. The only way to truly get answers is to call. So call already!

"Hello?"

"Hi, is this Taylor?"

"Yes."

"This is Chloe Hart. My mom said you called?"

"Uh, sh–she did?"

"Yeah, she said you called just a few minutes ago and wanted me to call you back at this number."

"Are you sure?"

"Are you saying you didn't call me?"

"Um, no. Why would I call you?"

Ouch. I felt like I'd been kicked in the stomach. "Taylor, if this is some sort of joke—"

"Just because I give you a hard time every now and then doesn't mean I'm the type of guy who would joke like this."

"You mean someone else called and left your . . . you've gotta be kidding me. I've been totally hoaxed! Who in their right mind would do this? Look, I've gotta go." I heard him snicker. "Wait, are you laughing?" *That little . . .*

"No." More snickers.

"Taylor . . ." I growled.

"Okay, yeah, I am. You have to admit this is pretty funny."

Funny? "You would think so, since I am positive it's your fault."

"My fault? How can this be my fault?" More chuckles.

"You're a smart guy, figure it out."

"Wait, you're serious, aren't you? You truly believe somebody who wanted to play some sort of prank on you, would do so because of me?"

"Yes." *Duh.* "Look, Taylor, this has been fun and all, but I need to go."

"Wait. Before you go, will you at least explain yourself?"

I was beginning to lose my cool. "You know what? I can't deal with this. You think everything is a game. Don't worry. I won't call you again."

"You can't hang up like that. Tell me what's going on in that fiery little head of yours."

"See what I mean? This is a joke to you, isn't it?"

"Chloe Elizabeth Hart, if you hang up this phone without telling me what in the world you're talking about—"

Elizabeth? "How did you know my middle name? No one knows my middle name." *This is such an invasion of privacy. There has to be a law against this!*

"I have my sources, and if you don't fess up I'll be sure to call you that from now on."

Blackmail? What, are we in junior high now? How in the world did this day go from bad to worse? This has got to end, and if the only way to make sure it happens is to sit on this phone a couple minutes longer, then—

"Fine! Don't you see that every time you talk to me it causes people to think things they don't need to be thinking? And I'm not talking about me, either—I'm talking about the whole student body, now gossiping about—about this, this . . . situation! When you draw attention to me, then *everyone* assumes I am free game to torment, which apparently has already begun, hence this phone call. You just came back today. Holy cow, Taylor, if this keeps up I can't imagine what people will think to do to me next. Thanks to you and your mocking, I am fast becoming the biggest freak in this school!"

"Let me get this straight," Taylor said. "You're angry with me for flirting with you?"

"Bingo. He has a brain cell."

"A brain cell? What is that supposed to mean?" Disbelief and resentment colored his voice. "You've got a lot of nerve, princess."

"Don't you dare call me prin—!"

"There are a whole lot of girls that would love to have the attention you got today."

"Of all the egotistical things to—"

"But I chose to focus on you," Taylor interrupted again. "Mainly because I thought you were more fun and lighthearted than you apparently are. In case you are not aware, I have a girlfriend."

"You—!"

"So if this is some sort of twisted excuse to make me see you differently and fall in love with you, then the game is up."

This is like talking to a rock. I can't believe I'm allowing myself to be insulted by a stupid, stubborn rock! Calm down, Chloe. Keep your voice calm. Deep breath. There. "Taylor Anderson, I am only going to say this one time, so listen carefully. You can have Anne. She's yours. As a matter of fact, you can have any girl in the whole flippin' town, for all I care. Except me. So seriously, don't even flatter yourself."

"Chloe, wait!"

I didn't even bother to say goodbye before I hung up the phone. *Jerk! Stupid, selfish, unreasonable imbecile!* I let out a weary sigh and began rubbing my temples to try to release the mounting pressure. *This isn't working.* As I opened my eyes, I glanced at the clock.

"Oh, no. Claire! I'm late." I grabbed the keys to Mom's Volvo and scooped up my purse, then yelled, "Bye, Mom!" and dashed out the door.

Reeling over the unbelievable conversation I'd just had with Taylor, I nearly collided with the neighbor's trash can as I backed up the car. *This is so Taylor's fault. First he makes me late, and then he tries to distract me so I almost crash the car. I wonder if I could sue. I cannot believe the ego that guy has, seriously thinking I was trying to trap him into falling in love with me. As if!*

After I sped out of the driveway, I felt something wet on my cheek. "What in the—?" I touched my face and realized and I was crying. *For crying out loud, Chloe. What are you crying for?* I laughed at the double meaning. *You're just angry, that's all. Sheez.*

My twelve-year-old sister, Claire, was waiting for me on a bench just inside the door of Chavez Ballet Studio. "For your information, Mom usually picks me up at 4:15, not 4:30," she announced as I opened the studio's front door. "It's not good to be late, Chloe. It makes you seem undependable to people."

Only half listening, I began to follow her to the car.

"If this keeps up, no one will be able to trust you." At the car, Claire turned around and waited for me. Then she surprised me by asking, "Chloe, have you been crying?"

"Yes."

"Why?"

"A stupid boy."

"Oh, I see. I've decided I'm never going to have a boyfriend. I find that boys are complete nuisances and idiots, set out and determined to make girls cry. Plus, I don't want to go through the pains of childbirth."

"What?! Er, uh, I don't think any woman does."

"Yeah, well, since technically you need a boyfriend to find a husband to have kids with, my goal is going to refrain from ever getting one." With that, she climbed into the car.

"Refrain?" I stared at her from the driver's seat.

"It means when you don't do—"

"I know what it means, Claire."

"Oh."

I started the car and pulled out of the parking lot.

"Oh! I almost forgot," Claire said. "Ms. Chavez says you can have your old job back anytime you're ready. Everybody misses you."

"Uh, well, I'll think about it."

Actually, when we'd moved from Denver, I had given up my dream of becoming a ballerina. Moving to a much smaller city had its advantages, but if you know more than your ballet teachers do, it doesn't work so well.

Ms. Chavez was so impressed with my ballet skills that she'd offered me a job as soon as I turned fifteen. I had taught for her for over two years, until last summer when the opportunity to work for a professional theater group came along. They were in need of background dancers for their musical. The idea appealed to me—working all summer dancing on stage, meeting new people every night. I really wanted to try something new and exciting, and getting paid for it was just icing on the cake.

While I worked at the ballet studio, I met Jordan and his girlfriend Kate, and they helped me learn all sorts of dance moves. They were professional ballroom dancers, so it was like getting really good lessons for free. Since they were both in the musical, I got to teach them a few ballet moves to help make their spins and lifts a bit easier and more fluid. We also became great friends in the process.

Thinking about it now, I realized I missed ballet. Even though my little sister still took lessons at the studio, I'd never really thought of working there again, but maybe I should. I sure loved teaching the littlest girls. The four- and five-year-olds were so sweet and innocent, and all of them dreamed of becoming famous ballerinas. I loved helping them create that reality. So even if I didn't jump on the job opportunity right away, it was something to think about.

"Hey, Chloe!" Carson called as he walked up to me. I was talking to his brother about the run we had finished where Ethan had just soundly beaten the other four-wheel-drive vehicles. Ethan and I were both kneeling on the dirt, comparing his tire treads. "I've got someone who wants to be introduced to you," Carson said to me. He turned and yelled toward a group of guys, "Yo, Blake!"

"Yeah?" a blond guy called back. He was tall and good-looking.

Carson motioned toward me. "I've got Chloe here to meet you."

Ethan and I stood up and brushed off our jeans. "I forgot Blake's been asking about you since we got here," Ethan said. "You'll like him—he's an easygoing guy."

Blake said something as he broke away from the group and started toward us. *Wow, is he hot!* I thought he'd be my age, but as he got closer I saw he was probably nineteen or twenty.

"Hi." He grinned at me.

My heart was beating so fast that if it had wings it would've fluttered away. *He's got dimples! Guys should never have dimples. They get away with everything when they do. Breathe, Chloe.*

"Chloe, this is Blake Winter. He just moved here from Boulder, Colorado. His truck's the nice black one over there." Carson nodded toward the parked vehicles. "Blake, may I introduce you to Chloe Hart, the prettiest, craziest, and funniest girl in the West?"

"You forgot to mention orneriest, feistiest, and meanest." Ethan smirked. "Don't be fooled by that sweet smile. She's inherited her red hair and temper naturally." Ethan and Carson both burst into guffaws.

"Hey, I prefer to be described as sassy." I smiled as I looked up at Blake.

"Hart, eh? So, are you the queen of hearts?" he teased.

"A lady never reveals her secrets. But if I must be a queen, then I want to be the queen of four-wheeling."

Carson laughed. "Chloe, the four-wheeling queen!"

"Why don't you want to be the queen of hearts?" Blake asked me.

"Because that's boring. I would much rather be known for something more fun and adventurous."

"Make way for the queen," Carson announced as he dragged me away from Blake and presented me to the rest of the guys. "Here's Chloe, the four-wheeling queen."

I glanced back. Blake was staring at me.

The guys all laughed and elbowed each other while they attempted to bow as well as they could on the uneven dirt. Then one of the guys, Jacob, surprised me by asking, "So, Queen Chloe, what are ya doing Saturday night?"

"Why?" I asked hesitantly.

"Because I really want to see the new Ryan Reynolds action movie, and you scream louder than any of the other girls. It'll make the movie more exciting if you go."

Oh, that's just great.

Jacob walked toward me. "So what do you say? You comin'?"

"Sorry, Jacob." The sound of Blake's deep voice behind me tingled all the way down my spine, and then frizzled back up to the ends of my ponytail. "I believe Chloe's going out with me on Saturday."

Raising my eyebrow, I turned around to face him with hands on my hips and challenged, "Really? You think so, do you?" Blake's dimple made an appearance and I was lost. "Well, if you're serious, then you've have to come over Friday and meet my parents. I can't go on a date with someone until my folks approve."

"I'll be there. What time?" His warm, chocolate-brown eyes sparkled right into mine.

"Better come for dinner," I managed to squeeze out of my suddenly dry throat. "Get my number from Carson or Ethan, then give me a call later and we'll work it out." I scanned the crowd to keep myself from staring too long into Blake's disconcerting eyes. I settled on Jacob.

"Okay, so if Blake's going to be with you Friday night and Saturday night," Jacob said, "then you've got to come with me Saturday afternoon. Besides, I've already met your parents, remember?"

I giggled. "Okay, okay, I'll come."

FIVE

♥

WINDS OF CHANGE

Thursday morning when I walked into the main building to head to my history class, all glorious thoughts of Blake Winter skipped my mind. The first fission of doubt on this "perfect day" had begun. Everyone was whispering to each other in the halls.

"Did you hear . . . ? Taylor . . ."

Or, "Taylor Anderson . . . girlfriend . . ."

"His phone call . . . Taylor . . . not happy . . ."

What is going on? Suddenly, I was brought back down to earth as I remembered the phone call from the day before. Determined not to panic, I slid into my seat at the front of the room.

By the end of my second-hour health class, I had heard enough to realize my name wasn't connected to the Taylor gossip. That's when I knew something major had happened to him yesterday that had nothing to do with me.

It was all over the school by the time my art class rolled around. Everyone was talking about it, and no one felt the need to whisper anymore.

"Did you hear?" Emma Bradford gushed to her tablemates as she set out her art supplies. "Taylor Anderson got dumped by his girlfriend last night. Isn't that *so* exciting?"

I gasped as I turned to Madison and Alyssa, who were getting their pastels ready before the bell rang. They must've heard the news already, because they both nodded their heads at my stunned look. "You're kidding." I felt horrible. *Why do I feel so horrible? I wonder which phone call he got first, mine or hers? No way. I totally forgot to tell Maddi and Alyssa about the phone call!*

The bell rang just as Taylor entered the room. No one even bothered to whisper while they talked about him. He glanced around the class and made a sort of rueful smile at the twittering girls, who faked looks of sympathy.

Wow, how happy can people get over his failure?

He must have read my mind, because at that moment our eyes locked. As he approached our table he hesitated, then quietly asked if it was okay for him to join us. I guess he was desperate enough to seek out the only safe haven in the room, and ironically, that was next to me.

My heart isn't made of stone, but it was definitely different to feel compassion for Taylor Anderson. Besides, no matter what he said to me yesterday, none of that compared to this. I half smiled as I pulled out his seat in response to his question. Relief showed on his face as he sat down next to me.

"Thanks," he whispered. "I know how hard that was for you, so thank you."

Surprised, I looked right into his eyes. He looked exhausted. There was a scant eight inches between us, and for a few moments I just stared at him. The normally lighthearted, sky blue orbs were now a dull grey blue. My heart lurched as we shared one of those life-changing moments that happen when you least expect them, when enemies claim truce.

Ms. Bailey's role call broke the spell. After a hurried, "Don't worry about it," to Taylor, I glanced up to see that Alyssa and Madison hadn't missed a beat. Thankfully, neither of them said anything, even though they were clearly dying to know what was going on. I could tell we would have a long talk soon.

Zack's little sister, Emma, was the first girl to "happen" by our table and nonchalantly drool over Taylor's artwork. "Wow. You are *so* talented. I wish I could draw like that."

I rolled my eyes when I saw that all Taylor had managed to do was a rough pencil sketch of the landscape we were all supposed to create with pastel chalk. Since this was his first full day back at school, he had a lot of catch-up work to do.

Anyway, I couldn't believe it, but one by one, every girl in the class made it over to our table. Even though Taylor seemed a bit annoyed by the constant interruptions, I have to say he handled it all like a pro. Not one of those girls knew when she left our table that she had unwillingly caused him more pain by her actions. In fact, Taylor did such a good job smiling and small-talking back that each girl probably felt extra special and loved. *I bet I know what they'll be telling their friends after school,* I thought. I had to admit the guy was charming.

Even Alyssa and Madison were not immune when he complimented them on their choice of subject or color. This became apparent as we were walking out of the classroom together and Madison asked, "I wonder who the next Miss Taylor Anderson will be?"

Without thinking, I answered, "Good grief. Can you imagine what she'd have to put up with? The last thing I would want to be is popular. Sure, having friends is cool, and having a lot of friends is even better. But to have to be constantly in the spotlight because you're part of the 'in' crowd? Er, no thank you. My stint on stage was limited just to dancing, and personally, I would like to keep it that way."

Madison was the first to catch my blunder. "So you're worried Taylor will ask you to join him, huh?"

"What? No!"

"Methinks she protests too much," Alyssa said, misquoting Shakespeare.

"Ha ha, you two," I replied as we maneuvered our way through the crowded hallway. "You don't know the half of it. I was so busy describing every detail of Blake this morning that I forgot to mention about the phone call I had from Taylor yesterday."

Alyssa's "What? You're kidding!" was overpowered by Madison's "No way!"

"Yep. I wasn't home when he called, and I had an urgent message to call him back on his cell phone."

Madison gasped. "Shut up. You have Taylor Anderson's cell number?"

"Yeah." *Wait, I think I do. Did I throw it away?*

"Tell us quick what happened. Did you call him back? What did he want?" Alyssa said as we approached my English class.

"It was a prank. Someone else posed as him and left his number, so when I called it was actually really embarrassing."

Alyssa nearly choked. "What? Why would someone do that?"

"Was he nice about it?" Madison asked. "I mean, I imagine him just laughing it off, you know. He's always so happy."

Okay, now I feel really guilty. "Yeah, he was nice. Really nice. I was mad, though, and totally lost my cool. It ended up getting ugly—you have no idea. I blamed the whole thing on him, and then he said stuff to me. Anyway, we got into a big fight."

Alyssa sighed. "Chloe, I can't believe you didn't say anything to us sooner. You—"

"So that explains that look you two shared," Madison interrupted. "I have to say from where I sat, it was a pretty intense."

"Yeah," Alyssa said. "I know you really like Blake and all—plus he sounds amazing!—but I have to say there's some serious chemistry between you and Taylor."

Whatever. "Y–you're crazy. Too much romantic drama for one day can leave everybody on the edge of their seats. Besides, even if I wanted him—which I don't—there is no way Taylor likes me or ever will like me. Mark my words he'll have another cheerleader girlfriend within a couple of days."

"Uh, guys?" Madison said. "When did the bell ring?"

I looked up and glanced around the empty hall. We had stopped walking about five feet from my classroom door, which was shut. Everyone else was in class. "Uh-oh!"

"Bye!" Madison and Alyssa chimed, then hurried toward their classes.

I sneaked through the door and grabbed an empty desk in back. A few people noticed me, but no one decided to nark me out.

"Thanks," I mouthed to a couple of the students and then shrugged at Ethan's questioning look. I glanced to the front of the room. Mr. Young was proficiently writing a novel on the blackboard. As I hastily removed my AP World English book from my backpack, a folded piece of paper fell out of it. *What is that?* I leaned over and picked it up. On the outside it read:

For: C. Elizabeth H.
From: T. Darcy A. ← *There, now u know my middle name, so we're even.* ☺ *Blackmail, only IF necessary.*
PLEASE KEEP SECRET.

You've got to be kidding me. He must've sneaked this in during art class. Quickly, I slouched down in my chair and glanced back at Mr. Young, who was still furiously writing. I opened my English book, unfolded the note, and placed it inside the book. Snuggling the book next to me, I pretended to be totally engrossed in English literature.

Dear C,

First I would like to apologize for being such a jerk on the phone yesterday. I shouldn't have said what I said. Honestly, I didn't mean it. It was just the heat of the moment. Do you ever wish you could just rewind sometimes and start over?

Right after you hung up, I received another phone call from Anne. She'd had her own call from someone (maybe the same person who called your house?) who told her that not only had I been flirting with you at school, but they also made up some crazy story that I was cheating on her with you. I won't go into all the gory details— just believe me when I say they were bad.

I kept trying to get Anne to listen to me. But after a good thirty minutes of listening to her rant and rave and viciously attack someone she didn't know, someone who I explained didn't do anything, I decided it was time to break up with her. How can I have a girlfriend who won't trust me?

I am writing this as a warning, I guess, because what you said last night was true. People talk about me and

whatever happens to me. It's kind of annoying, I know.
I'm sorry to put you in the middle of it all. I will find who
did this. But until then, I wanted you to know the real
story behind all the other stories you'll hear today.

Thanks for reading.

So sorry,
T

"Miss Hart? Excuse me. Ahem. Miss Hart!"

"What?" I jerked forward. As I sat up, I almost dropped my English book in the process. Mr. Young and the rest of the class were staring right at me. *Oh, no! I've been caught.*

"Would you like to share what you were reading just now with the class, Miss Hart?" Mr. Young leaned up against his desk with his arms folded and waited.

"No, sir." I gulped. *Please don't make me read it.*

"Miss Hart, are you aware of the rules in this room?"

"Um, yes." I glanced over and caught Ethan winking at me. I think he thought it would make me feel better. It didn't.

"Then you do realize that if you don't read that letter out loud to the class, you must forfeit it to me?"

"Yes, Mr. Young."

"By not reading it, you will also have to face any consequences I choose to give you. Are you willing to face anything I give you, or would you rather read it now?"

"I'm willing to face the consequences."

"That must be one very interesting letter, Miss Hart."

"Yes."

"Bring it here, Miss Hart," Mr. Young commanded, holding out his hand.

Jenni James

Slowly, I walked to the front of the room. I could hear snickers and whispering behind me. Red-faced, I handed Mr. Young the letter and watched as he read it silently to himself. *Can this get any more mortifying?*

"You're correct," he said. "This is a very interesting letter. Should I share it now with the rest of the class?"

"No. Please don't."

"Look at how curious the class is. I want to remind you that if you can't give me a good excuse why I shouldn't share this with the class, I will read it to them anyway."

"Please, Mr. Young, I'll do whatever it is you want— detention, extra homework, whatever—just please don't read that note out loud." I was getting desperate. I couldn't even face the class.

"Why not, Miss Hart?"

I looked him in the eye. "If you do, it could hurt someone, someone other than myself. It is my fault for reading that in here when I knew better and knew the rules. Completely my fault. I would hate to have someone get hurt because I was impatient. Please, please, please punish me, but don't punish someone who doesn't deserve it." My hands had begun to shake. I held my breath for Mr. Young's answer.

He took off his glasses and rested them on his receding hairline, then rubbed the bridge of his nose. "Congratulations, Miss Hart. In the last eight years I've taught at this school, no one has ever given me an excuse as worthy as that one." Half of his white mustache rose into a smile, and I nearly died of relief. "Your secret is safe," he said. The class erupted in groans. "I do however, expect you here precisely at 3:00 this afternoon."

Oh my gosh, I think I'm gonna cry. "No problem. Thank you, Mr. Young." I headed back to my seat.

"Oh, and Miss Hart?"

"Yes?" I turned around to face him.

"Please don't be late for class like you were today." The other students burst out laughing.

"Yes, sir." *Nothing like trying to stay hidden. Sheez, this guy doesn't miss anything.*

As soon as the last bell rang at 2:55, I was out the door and headed toward Mr. Young's classroom. I hadn't had a chance to tell Alyssa and Madison about my punishment yet. They would probably be waiting for me, but it was too late now. I definitely didn't want to upset Mr. Young more by showing up late because I'd tried to find my two best friends. This was one of those frustrating moments when I wished my parents would relent and let me have my own cell phone. Their overprotectiveness was pretty annoying. After all, didn't cell phones actually save lives? When I scurried into the classroom, I noticed I had two minutes to spare. *Phew.*

"Welcome back, Miss Hart. Please come in and have a seat." Mr. Young pointed to a desk at the front of the room. I nervously sat down. "If you don't mind, we'll wait just a moment," he said. "I'm expecting another visitor."

Obviously, someone else had gotten in trouble today too. But what if I had to sit through detention or something? *Oh, no,* I thought suddenly. *I can't make Alyssa and Madison wait that long. I'm going to have to call my mom to come get me.* "Mr. Young? How long am I going to be here?" My voice sounded squeaky like it always did when I was nervous.

"Just a minute, Miss Hart. That is still to be determined."

Oh, please, I hope I get off for good behavior.

Mr. Young looked behind me, then smiled and exclaimed, "Welcome to the class, Mr. Anderson. Would you please take a seat next to Miss Hart?"

I whipped my head around and saw Taylor standing there. *What? Oh, kill me now. This is by far the most humiliating day of my life!* I could tell by the questioning look Taylor gave me that he had no idea what this was about. I couldn't make up my mind if that was good or not.

"Mr. Bradford, if you would be so kind as to shut the door and to wait outside," Mr. Young said.

Zack's here too? I glanced at Taylor, who looked back at his friend and shrugged.

"I promise you will see your friend alive and safe in a moment. Thank you," Mr. Young said just before Zack closed the door.

SIX

♥

DETENTION OR NOT?
THAT IS THE QUESTION!

Mr. Young cleared his throat. "Well, first I must say thank you for coming. And yes, Miss Hart, I will be informing Mr. Anderson of what happened today. Welcome to consequences."

Beyond mortified, I could feel Taylor watching me as I leaned forward and put my head in my hands, wishing I could just hide there until it was over.

"Mr. Anderson, do you recognize this?"

From the corner of my eye, I saw the teacher hand Taylor the note. I have to admit that apart from a slight gasp, Taylor barely betrayed any emotion at all, even though he had to be as sickly stunned as I was.

"Yes, sir, I wrote it," he replied.

At least he's honest . . . or brave. I couldn't decide which.

The teacher chuckled. "So your middle name is Darcy, Mr. Anderson?"

That is so cruel. Mr. Young is way Old School. I sat up in my chair and looked over at Taylor, but he didn't meet my eyes.

I am so sorry, Taylor, I thought. *If there was anything I could take back, it would be this moment. No, it would be reading that note in class.*

"Yes, Mr. Young. I was named after my great-grandfather, Darcy Taylor."

"I see," the teacher said. "Well, that is nothing to be ashamed about, son."

Taylor looked up. "Yes, I know. I just don't like people making fun of him, you know?" He glanced briefly at me and then back at his desk.

What kind of consequence is this? Is this some sort of reverse psychology, making me watch this guy get tormented? Okay, I get it. I'll never *read another note in class, ever.*

"Well," Mr. Young went on, "it seems we have a problem. Miss Hart was caught reading your letter in my class today. As you are well aware of, Mr. Anderson, I have consequences for students who refuse to read a letter to the rest of the group. Of course, this never stops me from reading the note out loud anyway."

I looked up at Taylor, but he was staring at his desk and chewing on his lower lip.

"Mr. Anderson, in eight years, every letter or note I have found in my class has been read to everyone."

From Taylor's expression, I could tell he was mortified that the whole school would soon know all about the letter. *This is the most brutal lesson ever!*

"Until now," Mr. Young said.

Confusion and disbelief flashed across Taylor's face as he glanced back up at the teacher.

"Yes, Mr. Anderson. Miss Hart's reason for not reading to the class out loud was not because she was embarrassed for herself, which I'm sure she was." Mr. Young paused and looked down at me. "She was concerned for you, Mr. Anderson."

I stared at my desk and felt my face turn red. *Oh, no, I'm blushing. Don't blush. Don't blush.*

"Miss Hart did not want you to feel the aftermath and gossip that would no doubt have come from reading it. To put it in her own words, 'I would hate to have someone get hurt because I was impatient.'"

Please let me die right now. Please.

"Mr. Anderson, I asked you to come here this afternoon to make you aware of this young lady, who will now be sitting in detention until 4:30 p.m. on your behalf."

Four thirty! I have to be here until 4:30? Mom is so gonna kill me.

"No, she's not."

Taylor's statement caught me by surprise, and I think it shocked Mr. Young, too.

"Oh . . . oh really?" he sputtered.

"I'll stay—"

"Taylor—" I interrupted.

"Mr. Young, it was my fault. I owe her one anyway."

For the second time that day, I found myself staring into Taylor's eyes. Except this time they were sky blue and full of relief. But I still wasn't convinced he was making the right choice. "Thanks, Taylor, but you don't have to do this."

"On the contrary, Miss Hart," Mr. Young interjected. "I find this very enlightening and magnanimous. It gives us insight into Mr. Anderson's character, and it is the correct and gentlemanly thing to do. In my day, a gentleman was always allowed to be a gentleman. Therefore, Miss Hart, you are free to go and enjoy the rest of your afternoon."

"But—"

"Go, Chloe. I don't have a carpool waiting for me like you do," Taylor said. "I have my own car to get myself home when

Jenni James

this is over. Besides, I have a ton of homework to catch up on, so really, it's okay. Just go."

He did have a point. Now I wouldn't have to have my Mom come and rescue me, or make Alyssa and Madison wait any longer. "Thanks." I smiled. *Karma can be good sometimes.*

"We're even." Taylor grinned. "Oh, could you tell Zack to head off without me? Let him know I'll talk to him tonight, okay?"

"Sure, no problem. And Taylor? There's one more thing. About the phone call, I'm really sorry I lost my cool like that. It was, as you said, in the heat of the moment."

"You mean you're usually much nicer when you tell people off?" he teased.

"Something like that. Sorry."

"Forgiven. Am I?"

"I don't know, we'll have to see." I grinned and winked before I turned to Mr. Young. "Thanks. I, uh, have definitely learned my lesson."

"No more notes in class?" His twinkling eyes belied his gruff voice.

"No more notes ever." I headed for the door.

I found Zack on a bench at the end of the hallway. He was listening to some music on his iPod and bouncing a basketball to the beat. With his eyes closed, jamming to the rhythm, he looked like he could hold his own on any court. I could definitely see what Alyssa saw in him.

He didn't hear me the first couple of times I called out to him. Finally, I walked right up to him and touched his shoulder. "Zack?"

"Uh, yeah?" He quickly removed one of the earpieces and turned down the volume. "Sorry. Did you need something?"

"Taylor wanted me to tell you he'll be in Mr. Young's class until 4:30. He said you could go ahead and he'll talk to you

58

later tonight." I began to walk away, but to my amazement Zack started to follow me.

"No way. Is he in trouble or something?"

"No. Actually, he was rescuing me."

"Really? Sounds like Anderson, always helping the ladies." Zack fell into step with me. "Um, you're Chloe Hart, right?"

I wonder if this is leading to Alyssa. "Yep," I said as I walked toward the hallway door.

"Oh. Do you have a friend named Alyssa Ming?"

Man, I'm good.

Zack opened the door for both of us. "She plays the cello," he added when I didn't answer right away.

"Yeah, I'm hoping she's still waiting for me."

"Wait, you're heading to her right now?" Zach asked.

I smiled. "It's more or less her car I need, but she should be there too."

"Hey, uh—can I walk with you?"

If I didn't know better, I'd think Zack Bradford sounded a bit shy. "Sure. If you want to." I shrugged.

As we headed across the lawn toward the parking lot, I saw Alyssa and Madison lounging against the side of Alyssa's car. Madison noticed me first.

"Hey, Chloe! Where've you been?" she shouted.

"Mr. Young's," I yelled back. "Alyssa, I've got a surprise for you."

She did a double take as we I walked closer. "Zack? Is that you? I thought you were Ethan."

"Yeah, I get that a lot." He grinned as we approached the girls. "Hey, uh, I was wondering if, if . . ." —he looked at all of us and then back at Alyssa— "if you'd like to walk with me for a minute."

"Sure." Alyssa beamed and wiggled her eyebrows at us as she passed.

Madison and I watched her and Zack walk over to some shade trees on the lawn. We smiled at each other. It was about time the guy made a move.

"So, I heard you had a more-than-interesting letter during English today, one that you refused to share with anyone." Madison's tone was full of meaning. "Don't look at me like that. Everyone's been talking about it."

I sighed. "Yeah. I have to say, Chloe has learned a lot today."

"You have, huh? Would it have anything to do with a certain note someone wrote you?"

"Actually, it has a lot to do with it. A whole lot."

"Okay, spill. I'm dying already!"

So, of course I did what any best friend with a good three-year standing relationship would do. "All right, but first you have to promise me not to tell anyone. Promise?" *Except Alyssa, of course.* It went without saying that Alyssa was exempt from secrets.

"Not a soul," Madison said. "Now talk."

Which I did. I told her everything—except, well, the Darcy part. That really wasn't my secret to share anyway.

"I can't believe how harsh Mr. Young was. I mean, you are so lucky that Taylor is as great as he is."

"It was weird, Madison. He was really cool about it, considering yesterday with my phone call and then his girlfriend right after me."

"So let me get this straight. Taylor broke up with his girlfriend because of you, right?"

"What? No . . . no!"

"But didn't the note say he was angry with Anne for attacking you?"

"Yeah, well, but he meant because she didn't trust him," I explained.

"So *then* he fills in for you on your detention?"

"Yeah, well, yeah, but—"

"And he apologizes, plus he admits that you were right."

"So? We were both right, and I way overreacted—"

"Hello!" Madison interrupted. "Can't you see what I see?"

"What?"

"What? That Taylor is totally into you, Chloe."

"Wha–at? No, not even. You're way off the mark there."

"Am I?"

"Madison, seriously—"

Just then, Alyssa came rushing back to the car, a shy smile on her face. Madison and I looked at each other, and then we both stared at Alyssa again.

"Well, did he ask you out?" Madison asked her.

Alyssa shrugged, then smiled and nodded furiously.

"Shut up!" Madison threw her arms out.

"Ahhhh!" We all went in for a major group hug.

"So are ya out *out* with him?" I couldn't help asking, just to clarify.

"Oh, no. Not *out* out, but we're going to a movie Saturday."

"That is so awesome. I am so happy for you!" I said. *Wow. Who'd have thought? Zack Bradford and Alyssa.*

"Hey, don't you have a date on Saturday too?" Madison asked.

"Holy cow, you're right. We've got to get home ASAP. Blake was supposed to call me this afternoon." I ran over to the front passenger door.

"What an amazing day," Alyssa said as she climbed into the driver's seat. "I don't think there will ever be a day as surprising as today."

Madison and I smiled at each other over the roof of the car, then climbed in ourselves. *Now if only there was someone for Madison.*

SEVEN

♥

MOM RULES THE ROOST

"No way!" I whined. "You can't make me go out with him." I stormed into the dining room. Of course, Mom followed me.

"Chloe Elizabeth, this is a nice thing to do. Stop being such a brat."

"I'm not. Mom, he's—"

"A little shy, that's all. Collin's mother is always telling me at our book-club meeting how wonderful she thinks you are—so smart and pretty—and how much she wishes her Collin would find a nice girl like you. So I just thought, what could be the harm in you two at least getting to know each other better? I swear, Chloe, if you don't go on this date, how could I ever face his mother again? It would be humiliating."

Why does she have to be so good at guilt trips? "Mom, but he's—he's, I don't know . . . weird."

"Chloe, I am not asking you to marry the guy, all right? One date, okay? One. You won't die, I promise." Mom sighed as she sat down at the dining room table. "This is something that children do for their parents and for their parents' friends, and that's that."

"But Mom, he talks about odd stuff and everybody always stares at him." I tried again. "I can't believe you would actually plan a date for me without even asking me!" Frustrated, I sat down on a chair facing her.

"You will be nice to that boy, Chloe. I mean it! Not one rude thing better come out of your mouth."

"You know I'll be nice to him. That's not the point. The point which you seem to be forgetting here is that you scheduled a date for me on a night when I already have one."

"Again, if you had talked to me and had written it on the calendar like you were supposed to, this wouldn't have happened."

"For crying out loud, Mom. This is Blake Winter we're talking about. He's coming over tomorrow to meet you guys, just so he can take me out Saturday night. And now I've got a date with Collin."

"Chloe—"

"A date my mother scheduled today after I had already promised Blake. What am I supposed to do?"

"This is not open for discussion, Chloe. You are going with Collin."

Cassidy chose that precise moment to saunter in. Personally, I thought it was pretty bold until . . . *I've got it!* "Why can't Cassidy go with Collin?" I pleaded, looking directly at my sister. "We could even double." *Come on, Cass, work with me!*

Cassidy giggled and began to gag. I pretended to hand her a brown paper bag, which she mimed throwing up in. It was an old joke of ours, but for some reason it never worked with Mom.

"Very funny, girls," she said, her face completely serious.

"Please, Mom. Me and Cass together?"

"Chloe, this is ridiculous. You know the rules. You know that your father and I won't allow anyone living in this house to date before they're sixteen. Cassidy, in case you have forgotten, is fifteen."

I rolled my eyes at Cass's unsympathetic "sorry" gesture. "No, I didn't forget. I thought maybe you'd make an exception, though. I mean, she looks seventeen, so no one would know." I tried one last time as Cassidy smugly waved goodbye to me behind Mom.

"His mother asked about you, Chloe. You're going with him."

Resigned to my fate, I moaned. "Fine. Blake left his number, right? I guess I'll call him back."

I grumbled under my breath as I picked up the phone and the slip of paper with his number. I carried them into my room, then plopped on the bed and started to dial.

"Hello?" he answered after a few rings.

"Hi, Blake, this is Chloe. Sorry I missed your call."

"No problem. I was wondering what time you wanted me over tomorrow for dinner."

"Well, 5:30, but—"

"Sounds good. I should be able to make it."

"Uh, well, that's the thing, I'm not sure you're going to want to make it." I plunged ahead before I lost my nerve. "Actually, I have some bad news. I mean, you're still welcome to come tomorrow . . . It's just that I can't go out with you on Saturday."

"Why not?"

This is so embarrassing. "Uh, my mom has gone all commando on me and totally set me up with this guy Collin, who drives me nuts. So I have to go with him instead of you, but could I maybe get a rain check?"

"You're kidding! Can't you beg or something?"

"Okay, yeah. Tried. Seriously, she is *so* like a war general sometimes. Right now she's been workin' the guilt factor. She's in this book club with his mom."

"Book club?" Blake sounded amused.

I'd take amused over mad or hurt any day. "Yep. And apparently my mom will never be able to show her face again if I back out, so . . ."

"So what's he like?

"Collin?"

"Yeah, a guy's gotta know his competition, right?"

"You think Collin is competition?" I blurted out.

"He's a guy, right?"

"Yes. I guess you could call him that."

"And he's going out with you instead of me," Blake said. "He's competition. So what's he like?"

"Oh. He's . . . er, I don't know. He's, like, not all there, you know?"

"Is he as good looking as me?"

"As you? Hmm. I guess he's cute, but more in a loner sort of way."

"Oh, well, cute? Cute, I got beat."

"You sure about that? Just because you've got dimples, don't think it's in the bag."

Blake groaned. "Don't remind me. I hate my dimples."

"What? Why? Every girl loves dimples."

"So you're saying you like them, then?"

"Uh, maybe."

"I'll take that as a yes." He laughed into the receiver, and I shuddered. There was something about his voice that turned my insides into jelly.

"So, do you still plan to come for dinner tomorrow?" I asked.

"I wouldn't miss it. What are your parents like?"

"Um, they're sort of crazy."

"Crazy?"

I laughed. "Well, they just like to put the guys who date me through some sort of a dating ritual thing."

"Dating ritual?" Blake sounded surprised. "What do you mean? What's it like? Is there anything I need to know?"

"Just go with it. You'll be fine."

"Okay, come on, Chloe. Can't you give me more than that?"

"You definitely need a sense of humor to survive."

"All right, so I need a sense of humor."

"The funnier you are, the better."

"Wait. You mean I have to act funny? Like a monkey or something?"

"What? No! You think you'll have to act like something?" I giggled.

"Very funny." I could hear the grin in his voice. "How else am I supposed to act?"

"Like yourself." Smiling, I got up off the bed and wandered over to my mirror.

"Myself?"

"Yep, be yourself and you'll be fine." I made a face at my haphazard hair.

"You know, you're lucky I'm brave or this could really begin to scare me," Blake said.

I wonder if he likes red hair. I sprung a curl and answered, "Scare you? No, it's not scary. Just, um, funny."

"So, you guys are going to make fun of me or something?"

"Maybe. I don't know. I never know what they're planning to do. Stop being so curious. I promise, you'll live." As I turned to plunk back on the bed, my knee collided with the corner of my dresser. *Ouch!* "Oh, sh–sugar!"

"Sugar? Did you say sugar?" I could tell Blake was trying not to laugh.

"Not always."

"Oh?"

"No. Sometimes I say 'sugar plum fairies.'"

He snorted. "You say 'sugar plum fairies' instead of—"

"Don't say it!"

"—shoot."

"Oh, I thought you were going to say something else."

"I thought about it," he said.

"You did?"

"Yep, but I changed it at the last minute. I didn't want you to get mad and say 'sugar' or something."

"Ha ha. Good one."

"So why don't you say, uh, the other word?"

"Oh, because—"

"Because of your parents?"

"No. Well, yeah, but mostly because I'd rather be unique and different than follow the crowd." *Oh my gosh! What am I saying? Blake is* so *going to think I'm a dork now.* "Anyway, I know it's kind of childish to say 'sugar,' but I always have, so it's—"

"Chloe!" my mom yelled.

Thank you, Mom. "Uh, Blake, I've gotta go. My mom's calling me."

"Sure. I'll see you tomorrow."

"Okay. See ya tomorrow. Don't forget to be funny. Bye."

"Bye. Oh, uh, Chloe?"

"Yeah?"

"Just for the record, I like that you're unique. Besides, it sounds cute when you say 'sugar.'"

My heart stopped and then flip-flopped. "Really?" *He thinks I sound cute?*

"Yes. And I'll see you tomorrow."

"Bye." I sighed and fell back onto my pillows as I hung up the phone. *A girl could kiss a guy like that.*

"Chloe Elizabeth!" My mother's exasperated shout sliced through my daydreams of kissing Blake.

"Coming," I called, wishing for just three minutes of privacy. It's not every day a girl gets told she sounds cute.

My mom was still in the dining room. She was sitting next to my dad.

"There you are, Chloe. Have a seat." Dad pointed to the chair opposite him.

Wondering if we were having some sort of family conference, I sat down hesitantly. "What's up?" My parents only did this gang-up thing if they needed to tell one of their kids something upsetting.

"Well I've just checked my email." Mom paused, obviously waiting for me to speak up. When I didn't, she went on, "It seems you were caught reading a note in your English class today."

You're kidding me. Mr. Young emailed my parents? That is so harsh. "Um, yeah. I was." *Great. So what's it going to be, grounding for life?*

"Your father and I" —she looked over at my dad as if to include him— "think it's time for you to take some responsibility."

"Okay."

"Four-wheeling instead of doing your homework, talking on the phone all evening, reading notes in class." My dad raised a finger for each of the things he listed, as if he was counting them off.

"So? What do you want me to do?"

"We think it would be a good idea for you to get a job. It's been almost three weeks since the theater group broke up. Playtime is over, Chloe." My mom gave me a knowing look.

{♥}

Needless to say, after the "talk" with my folks, I called up Ms. Chavez at the dance studio to ask for my old job back. She said I could start Monday. I asked for weekends and Wednesdays off so I could still go on dates, just in case a certain someone felt like asking me out again after this weekend's test and my blatant rejection of our first date.

My phone call with Ms. Chavez turned out to be a bit more lucrative than I'd expected. Not only did she offer to give me a raise, but she had a friend who was willing to consider me for Arizona State University's ballet scholarship program. I guess she had told her friend about me and the work I'd done in her studio. Ms. Chavez even offered to help me with an admissions DVD. To say my parents freaked would be an understatement, and I was pretty excited myself.

Later that evening when I called Madison to tell her about my date with Collin, my call to Blake, my new job, and my possible ASU scholarship, she still found time to insist Taylor liked me. But Madison was singing a different tune about Taylor on Friday. We all were, because apparently, he'd fallen in love.

EIGHT

♥

TAYLOR IS IN LOVE

So what else would the whole student body talk about besides Taylor Anderson? *You know, I have no idea, because it appears there is always some excitement that happens to revolve around him. Seriously, can't we think of something more original? So he's got a new girlfriend. Like that's a shocker. The longest the guy has ever gone girlfriendless was back in the seventh grade, and even that was for just three days.*

In seventh grade, rumor had it that the girl he wanted to add to his list of conquests was on a trip with relatives at the time, which is why it took three days. Of course, the story goes on to say that she did manage (after an urgent phone call from a friend who tipped her off) to convince her family to cut their vacation short so she could receive the wondrous honor of becoming Taylor's next.

Who does this? And seriously, what makes him so special that the whole world stops just for him? Okay, I'll admit it was chivalrous when he did my detention for me. Still, he is just a guy, isn't he? A guy who has a dreadfully annoying habit of bragging about his newest and latest model.

"And then we kissed. It was so awesome. I knew right then that I had to ask her to be mine." Taylor beamed.

Oh, spare me. It sounded as if he had gotten the lines right out of a B-rated soap opera. I rolled my eyes and I looked up from the single-minded focus of my chalk landscape. I wanted to see if anyone else had bought into Taylor's sappy drivel.

You've got to be kidding me. Half of the art room had surrounded our table. The other half had strained so hard to hear Taylor's account of how he found his *one* true love that they had to hang onto their respective tabletops to not fall off their seats.

"What did she say?" Alyssa asked. I glanced at her and realized she'd long forgotten the landscape she'd been drawing. Her elbows sat on the table where her work should've been. She sighed dreamily and rested her chin on her hands.

Madison wasn't as impressed as she was amused. She claimed she wasn't very romantic, though for some reason she sure liked to hear the latest and greatest romance gossip.

"She said yes, of course." Taylor laughed. "What else would she have said?"

"What else indeed," I muttered under my breath as I leaned in closer to my artwork.

"What was that, Chloe?" His voice in my ear did zilch compared to the shivers his warm breath caused. *No guy should ever breathe that close to a girl's ear. It should be illegal or something.*

As I turned my head, our noses nearly collided. For a few moments, I stared at that nose and those lips so close to my own before my gaze traveled up to his glittering eyes. I jerked back but realized I had just crossed the line of disinterested into very interested by the standards of any one of the students who had witnessed our display. To give Taylor credit—which I shouldn't have done in case it gave the impression I was even mildly okay with the jerk's existence—he looked just as confused and shaken as I did. A couple of seconds longer and I may have tried to kiss the guy. Infuriated with myself and my lack of ability to breathe, I decided to end this fiasco.

"Ms. Bailey, can you help me with this water?" I asked loud enough to be heard over the music that streamed into her earphones. "I can't seem to get my lake to look real."

Immediately the room became a flurry of activity as the students dispersed to their seats.

Ms. Bailey looked up, removed her headset, and glanced around the room as everyone scrambled. "What has been going on here?"

Because it was an advanced art class, Ms. B. usually left us to our own devices, which allowed her to work freely on her paintings. She was lenient to an extent, but even she wouldn't tolerate complete abandonment of work.

"Get back to work, now!"

She waited until all of the students were working on their landscapes before she walked over to our table. I felt a momentary stab of guilt and hoped the class wouldn't be punished.

"I'm sorry, Chloe. You were saying?"

"Oh, I was wondering if I could get some advice on my lake. I don't think it looks as realistic as it should."

"Remember, dear, you need to repeat the same landscapes and trees you see above the water, in the water. The same colors and all, just more muted, like this."

I looked over at Taylor, my mind wandering from Ms. B.'s demonstration. He was completely engrossed in his work. *He's probably trying to make up for all of the time he wasted boasting.*

A glance at Alyssa showed she was doing the same. Only Madison looked right back at me. Slowly, she raised one eyebrow. Her gaze left mine to settle on Taylor and then returned back to me. The look she sent spoke volumes.

Dang. She still thinks Taylor likes me. How am I ever going to convince her that he doesn't? Besides, Taylor's in love. Can't she see that?

{♥}

"Well, Mr. Winter, it says here that your parents are of German ancestry," my dad said as he read over the four-page questionnaire Blake filled out before dinner.

We sat around the table eating Mom's famous chicken pot pie. Dad had surprised us with the questionnaire earlier, but then he had the nerve to bring it to dinner, too. I still wasn't sure how Blake was handling it.

"Yes. My grandparents moved here from Germany." He bravely smiled.

"So was that before or after the war?" My father asked around a bite of broccoli.

"Uh, w–war?" Blake stuttered as he looked at me for help.

"Be funny," I whispered as I sipped some water.

"Yes, the war," my father said. "Did your grandparents migrate from Germany before or after World War II?"

"Oh, uh . . . before." Blake's eyes darted to my mom as she got up to refill her glass. He quickly scooped up a chunk of chicken.

"Well, that's good. Wouldn't want my daughter to date a Nazi."

Blake almost choked on the chicken. "Oh, uh, no sir."

Maybe he didn't hear me. I nudged Blake with my elbow to remind him again, but Dad was already talking.

"It says here that Lionel Anderson is your boss."

"Uh, yes. I work for him."

Wait a minute. Blake works for Taylor's dad?

"So you're working over at the hotel," my dad continued. "I assume that means you work in the housekeeping department. You're a maid, correct?"

Blake took a quick look at my father, probably trying to decide if Dad had just insulted him or not. "N–no, I'm not in housekeeping. I'm a concierge at the front desk."

Dad took another bite and flipped a page. "A concierge, huh? That is one fancy title. Does Lionel Anderson pay you enough?"

"Are you asking me how much money I make?" Blake's fork clattered to the table. He quickly picked it up and threw a panicked glance in my direction.

I smiled my most reassuring smile. *He just teasing you, remember?*

"Sure. If you want to tell me." Dad was eating this up. Literally.

For a split second, the room stood still. Blake stared at me and shook his head in obvious disbelief.

"Be funny," I mouthed.

Blake finally got it. He closed his eyes briefly. First one dimple appeared and then the other. He shook his head slightly and took another bite of pie, and I knew he was figuring out what to say. Finally, with smirk in my direction, he looked up at my dad and grinned. "Actually, sir, I feel I need to quit my job. It's not really helping me reach my future potential."

"What?" My dad seemed surprised. He set the questionnaire on the table next to his plate. "Excuse me? Did you say you wanted to quit? In this economy?" He raised his glass to his mouth.

"Yes. Even though I make a fairly decent living, I've always had this lifelong passion for garbage."

Dad nearly choked on his water. "W–what?"

Blake's expression was completely serious. "You see, ever since I was younger, I've always dreamed of becoming a sanitation engineer. There's nothing in the world that beats the hum of a large garbage truck, don't you think?"

It was after the pot pie and over the root beer floats that Mom and Dad learned Blake's real age, which was nineteen. I could tell they weren't too happy about it, but after Dad spit his water across the table and sprayed Blake's food, he wasn't in a position to grumble too loudly. Plus, it was obvious Blake was a nice guy with a job. Besides, he had dimples, which was all the incentive Cassidy and I needed to squeal in my room as we rehashed the evening later that night. We sat in our favorite spot on my bed, surrounded by decorator pillows and stuffed animals.

"He is so cute!" Cassidy said after a loud shriek.

"I know." I smiled and tucked my legs further underneath me.

"I can't believe he likes you, seriously." She flipped her curly blond hair away from her face. We had the same curls, except hers were—as she described them—golden. "If you ever get tired of him, let me know."

"Don't you think he's a little old for you?" I grinned as I watched her lean over to the dresser. She stole one of my hair ties and put her hair up.

"Whatever. If he was twenty-five and I was twenty-one, no one would even blink." Cassidy scrunched up her nose and fell back on the pillows. "It's not fair. Why can't I be older? I want to go on dates too—except not with Collin."

"Grr. I forgot about Collin." I tossed a pillow at her. Just hearing his name put a damper on the evening.

Why do I have to go out with Collin, especially when a guy like Blake asked me first? Life is so unfair.

NINE
♥
DATING FUMBLES

I was very proud of myself when I remembered my date with Jacob on Saturday afternoon. We went to see the new Ryan Reynolds movie, just like he'd said we would. And I tried not to scream when the scary parts came up, but I failed. Miserably.

Jacob clearly had a great time. He thought it was funny when I screamed. I'm not so sure the people who sat in front of us thought so, however. Since every time I screamed out in fear, I made them jump. Yes, sad but true. That is me. I am the person you can hear in the movie theater that yells or screams so loudly it actually scares everyone else. That's when people in front of you can get a bit hostile.

Needless to say, Jacob and I both survived the ordeal. Then I had to go on my date with Collin, where I spent the entire evening wishing I were anywhere else—even if it was back in that scary movie with Jacob and the scarier people in front of us.

I knew the date with Collin would be a disaster from the get-go. I mean, it's completely evident that you have an odd date when the guy actually asks you out through your mother. But does he have to sit there in public and continue to be odd? *Pardon me, but I thought the reason you took a girl out on a date was so you could get to know her a little more, not so you can play with your phone all night, studiously avoiding her.*

I let out yet another silent sigh as I watched my finger twirl around the rim of my glass of lemon water. We had ordered our food a few minutes before, but I knew it would be a wait due number of people at the restaurant. The Lion's Den is only the nicest one in our city—which figured, since Taylor's dad, Lionel Anderson, owned the place, just one of his many business ventures. I was a bit surprised at first when Collin pulled into the parking lot. It actually made me have some respect for him that he had thought to make reservations.

With another sigh, I moved my hand from the glass and began to refold the creases in my linen napkin again. The customers all around us were clearly having a marvelous time as they laughed and enjoyed each other's company.

With regret, I looked across the table at Collin and watched his face light up as he stared at his phone and read another email from one of his online friends. I wasn't sure he had any real friends, just online ones. Collin laughed. He must've read a joke. *He really does have a nice smile.*

When I had told Blake that Collin was cute, I wasn't kidding. Collin was really cute. Unfortunately, his personality and mannerisms needed some work.

Would it kill the guy to share with me what is so funny? It's like I don't exist. What was the point of taking me out, anyway? Frustrated, I glanced at my watch.

After another fifteen minutes, I had begun to feel a bit desperate and was debating whether or not I would be missed if I walked out the door—the same door that every three or four minutes released another happy couple to explore the world beyond this boredom. I enviously followed the progress of a young couple in their twenties as they departed. I was reminded briefly of Blake, which would've led to morose thoughts of a missed date had I been given the chance, which, unbelievably, I wasn't. Because as that couple left, someone else's arm held the door open for them, an arm my eyes soon discovered belonged to Taylor Anderson. His other arm was wrapped around the waist of Kylie, his new cheerleader girlfriend.

Oh my gosh! What is he doing here? What are the odds he would show up here tonight, of all nights?

I followed Taylor's progress across the room as he, with Kylie in tow, trailed the hostess to their seats. Many tables along the way were graced with his blinding smile and charm. I couldn't have been more grossed out by such a display. *Spare me.*

As Taylor neared our table, I quickly averted my eyes and proceeded to refold the napkin. *Oh, please don't let him recognize me. Don't let him recognize me.* For an instant, I was jealous that I had nothing else to occupy my hands like Collin did.

"Chloe Hart. Hello." *Dang.*

Reluctantly, I looked up into his amused eyes and faked a smile. "Oh, Taylor, hi. I didn't see you." In my nervousness, I accidentally brushed my napkin to the floor.

Taylor swiftly bent over and picked it up. As he placed the napkin in my hand, he held it and whispered in my ear, "Liar. You've been watching me since the moment I walked in." He squeezed my hand, then stepped back.

I felt my face heat up as Taylor swept Kylie toward Collin. I was speechless.

"Collin Farnsworth. Good to see you," Taylor said.

As he gaped at Taylor, Collin fumbled with his phone and dropped it. Then in a flash, he was up, pumping Taylor's hand.

"Taylor Anderson! What a surprise! So nice of you to come over."

"Oh, it's nothing." Taylor glanced back at me and grinned.

I rolled my eyes. *Could he be any more obnoxious?*

"Here." Taylor forcibly removed his hand from Collin's grasp. "Let me introduce you to Kylie." With his left hand he gently pushed her forward.

She looked a little less than thrilled to be introduced to Collin. But for Taylor's sake, she fulfilled the requirement like a beauty queen, all teeth and shiny lip gloss. In his obvious attempt to impress, Collin showered her with a load of gratuitous compliments. I was a bit embarrassed by his conduct and would've gotten over it eventually had Taylor not turned at that moment and grinned at me slyly. He glanced at Collin, then back at me and raised his eyebrows. All at once it hit me. *Taylor totally thinks I have a thing for Collin! Collin? As if!*

Immediately I began to pray they would leave soon, or our food would come, or the building would start on fire. Anything to escape Taylor's stupid "knowing" grin.

And then like manna from heaven, I was saved. Not the way I hoped, but who cares? Taylor's gaze left me long enough to catch Kylie's look. She seemed to practically beg to be out of our sight. All at once the gentleman in Taylor came alive. After a reassuring smile at Kylie, he turned back to me and Collin.

"Well, I'll let you two enjoy your night."

Yes! I was so happy, I could've hugged Kylie. Until—

"You've got yourself a great catch there, Farnsworth," Taylor said. "You hold on to her, all right?"

Collin looked at me—really looked at me for the first time that night—and then smiled. I could almost see the imaginary wheels turning. Suddenly, visions of repeated date nights just like this one popped into my head. Briefly, I contemplated causing Taylor bodily harm. Taylor patted Collin on the back like he would one of his buddies. Clearly proud of himself, he beamed right at me. *Why stop at bodily harm?*

Believe it or not, after that the date was even more boring, primarily due to Collin's excessive compliments of a certain "local celebrity" that I had to hear. To add insult to injury, after I had finally finished my meal, that little rat Taylor had the nerve to send over our bill, paid for by him, with a little note attached to the receipt that read: "We hope you enjoyed your romantic evening as much as we enjoyed ours. Love, Kylie and Taylor."

How long would it take for them to find Taylor's body? A long time, I bet. No one would really miss the guy anyway, right?

After church I pulled out my homework again and hit the books. I already had an essay to complete for English class, plus two paragraph worksheets for World History. I turned on my radio to a soft-rock station and plopped onto my bed. About forty minutes into ancient Rome, I had almost finished my second worksheet when Mom called me down to dinner.

My parents asked 101 questions about my date with Collin the night before. Talk about awkward. I mean, how do you tell your mom the guy she set you up with was a total pathetic loser, one who wouldn't even look twice at you until some popular jerk basically told him to? The worst part was that by the time Collin dropped me off he had almost convinced himself we were in love. *Good grief.*

Anyway, my family's dinner conversation went something like this:

MOM: So, how did your date with Collin go last night?

DAD: Yeah, how did that go?

ME: Uh, go? What do you mean?

MOM: Do you like him? Does he like you?

ME: What? No.

DAD: Why doesn't he like you?

ME: No. I mean, he likes me and all, he just doesn't *like* me.

MOM: Oh. So what did you talk about?

ME: Not much.

DAD: How much did the meal cost?

MOM: Honey, don't ask her that!

ME: I don't know.

DAD: A-ha! A good guy. He wouldn't let you see the receipt when he paid for it.

ME: Yeah, a true good guy. You have no idea.

CLAIRE: So was the food good?

ME: The food?

CASSIDY: Yeah. What did you order?

ME: Order?

CLAIRE: I bet it was awesome.

ME: You know, I can't remember . . .

MOM: There you go. If a girl can't remember the next day what she ate at the Lion's Den, then—

DAD: Then it isn't worth going there.

MOM: No, then she's in love.

ME: I am not in love! Eew. Look, can I go to my room now? I have a lot of homework.

MOM: Sure, honey. I'm glad you had a great time.

Parents. They so never get it, do they?

Had it not been for Blake's phone call that evening, I'm not sure I would've poked my head back out of my room until the morning. As it was, Blake completely cheered me up and brought me out of my grumpy mood.

"So, did you miss me while you were on your date last night?" he asked.

"Uh, what do you think?" I grinned.

"Yes. Definitely yes."

"Then you would be right."

"I would, huh? So how did it go?" I could hear the smile in his voice.

"Awful."

"Awful?" He sounded pleasantly surprised.

"Yes! Completely, totally, and utterly awful."

Blake chuckled. "So you missed me bad?"

"I was so desperate for conversation I would've talked to my fork. Except then people would've heard me talk to it."

"So you're saying the guy never talked to you?"

"No. It was so immature. All he did was play with his fancy Google phone."

"He's got a Google Nexus 5? Wow! What does his look like?"

What is it with guys and gadgets? "Blake, focus."

"Sorry." He sounded so sheepish I forgave him instantly. "So, you were saying you had a horrible date. How can I make it up to you?"

Ask me out on a date again. "Uh, I don't know."

"How about I take you somewhere amazing, somewhere really fun?"

I'm hooked. Seriously, is there a sweeter guy in the world? "Okay. When? Where?" I giggled.

"After four-wheeling Wednesday night? I already have that day off."

"Um, okay. I just have to be home by ten 10:00."

"Oh, yeah, you have a curfew," Blake said. "I forget that you're younger than I think you are."

"You do?"

"Yeah. You seem older to me, you know?"

Oh my gosh, he's so awesome. "I wish I was older."

"How old are you, anyway? Eighteen? Nineteen?"

"Really?" I giggled again. "I'm seventeen, weirdo."

He laughed his deep laugh. "Oh, someone just walked into the hotel. I've gotta go. I'll see you Wednesday then, okay?"

"Yep. It's a deal. I'll talk to you later."

"Bye." He sounded rushed.

"Bye." *A guy totally called me from work. How romantic is that?*

TEN

♥

LIFE GOES ON

By Monday it was official. School was now in swing. It was a full-fledged spiral of activity. The initial shock of the new school year was over—as far as teachers were concerned, that is. By the afternoon my homework load had doubled. It was all I could do to finish in time to make it to the dance studio a bit early.

My first class started at 5:00. I had hoped to get there at 4:00 to review a bit before the students came. As it was, the earliest I could get there was 4:30, which gave me just enough time to stretch before a little girl came in.

"Miss Chloe," she exclaimed as she ran to throw her arms around my knees. "You're back!"

It was the first welcome I'd had, since Ms. Chavez's class had already started by the time I showed up. I leaned over and hugged Gracie. "Hello, Gracie. I've missed you. How are you, sweetie?"

She ignored me completely as she turned back to face her mother. "See, Mom! I told you Miss Chloe would come back. I told you."

Mrs. Littleton chuckled. "Yes, you did. Glad to see you're back, Chloe. Gracie has really missed you."

"It's good to be back." I grinned. "Okay. Come on, missy. Let's get those slippers on."

"I'll be here in about an hour," Gracie's mom said.

Gracie and I told her goodbye before we hurried over to the bench to get ready.

Thank goodness my first class was a small, beginner one—there were only six children in the class. I actually got to review with them. By the time class was over, I had a rough idea of how I wanted to teach the intermediate class. They had continued on without me during the summer, so I used their hour to evaluate their skill levels.

Once 7:00 rolled around, I began to wonder why I had ever left the studio. The children from both classes were so excited to see me, it was like I was a celebrity or something.

The classes went by much faster than I expected them to. Before I knew it, it was time to go. I walked through the room and picked up a few stray items of clothing, then put away the stereo and the classical CDs. I grabbed my bag and put my jeans and T-shirt on over my tights and leotard. Next, I slipped my feet into my Vans and switched off the lights. I waved goodbye through the window to Mrs. Chavez as I passed the room where she was teaching adult tap dance. She quickly returned my wave.

As I walked toward the Volvo, I felt as if I had just started a new chapter in my life. I couldn't explain the feeling other than it was like a routine had just begun.

And begun it had. I had forgotten how busy life was when I had a job. The days and weeks passed unbelievably quickly, blurring together in a sort of pleasant monotony. I mean, there was an odd day here or there, like on the Wednesday when Blake took me dancing after four-wheeling. We didn't go anywhere—he just turned on his headlights and cranked up the radio. It was so wonderful to dance with him under the stars, even if it was on uneven ground and we laughed more than we actually danced. We stumbled and pitched into each other the whole time. It was a lot of fun and way more than made up for Collin's attempt at a date. Other than that, due mostly to conflicting work schedules, Blake and I hadn't been on a date again. And it was already October.

Even Taylor felt the stress of our senior year, and he buckled down more and actually completed his artwork on time. Of course, that didn't stop him from still, well, being Taylor. Apart from the initial tease session I knew was due on that first Monday after Collin's date, Taylor basically stopped taunting me and started boring us by bragging about Kylie Russell. But as much as that annoyed me, it was better than when he turned his attention toward me. As a matter of fact, it wasn't until plans for our annual Halloween party were announced that Taylor really remembered that Madison, Alyssa, and I existed, other than to act as the audience to his B-rated soap opera.

The Halloween party was all my friends and I could think about. We had lost track of time due to our hectic schedules—my dance classes plus filming and sending off my ASU admission DVD, Maddi's volleyball practice and games, and Alyssa's orchestra practice. So we only had a week to get the invites out or there wouldn't be enough notice for people to make it.

Not to brag or anything, but our Halloween parties had become a bit of a legend over the past few years. Well, in our crowd, that is. I'm sure none of the top tier of high school social hierarchy would've had much fun. Our parties are never something a reality TV show would be interested in filming. We're normal teenagers, okay? Normal teenagers whose parents would *kill* us if we dared to throw a party like that.

So, way back when I first moved to Farmington, Maddi, Alyssa, and I waited and waited to be invited to one of the cool parties. All summer long we waited. And then it was like a light bulb went off and we decided, why wait for something that may never happen? Why not host our own amazing party for everyone the popular crowd did not deign to invite to their parties? It was like an underground resistance—a boycott of the "in crowd," if you will—proof that you didn't have to be the coolest kid in school to have fun. Thus our annual themed Halloween party was born, and we'd had one for the last three years. One year, we all dressed up as pirates and went in search of real treasure. Madison's father had us split into teams and follow clues around the city. It was so cool. We got a lot of funny looks, but we didn't care. Maddi's father actually buried the treasure in the sand at one of the parks and we had to find it. Crazy, huh?

This year our theme was favorite vintage TV shows, and everyone was supposed to dress up as a character. We planned to have a lot of different games and contests that would revolve around the theme.

Since the party was at my house this year, it was my turn to make the invites. I had made a sample that looked just like a vintage TV. I brought it to show the girls in art so we could have time to really look it over and decide what needed to change. After Ms. Bailey called roll, I presented it with a flourish,

"Ta-da," I exclaimed as I dramatically dropped my attempt at a TV-shaped invitation on the table.

Madison, Alyssa, and even Taylor leaned over to see it. The TV screen read:

Madison, Alyssa, & Chloe's Annual Halloween Party
What's On: Vintage TV shows
Show Time: Friday, October 29, 7:00 p.m.

Station: Chloe's house
TV Directory: 4329 Meryton Street
Channel Dial: 555-5467
Advert: RSVP to advertise you're coming by the 19th

Alyssa gasped. "Wow, Chloe, that looks so awesome!"

"I love the way you used TV language instead of the 'where,' 'when,' and 'at' stuff," Madison said.

"Okay, um, what is up with the grey bobby pin and the tin foil at the tips?" Taylor asked.

"That's supposed to be a vintage TV antenna," I said defensively. "Get it? See, the bobby pin is spread out like a *V*."

Taylor chuckled. "I think it makes it look like a Martian."

"Don't listen to him, Chloe," Madison said. "Taylor's just jealous because he's not invited."

Surprisingly, Alyssa came to my defense too. "Yeah. He's a boy anyway. His opinion doesn't count. I think it looks fabulous."

Both girls mock-glared at Taylor until he gave up.

"All right, all right." He grinned as he raised his hands in a "don't shoot" gesture. "I can see when I'm out numbered." He turned to me and half bowed. "Chloe, I apologize. On second thought, it does look like a TV—*Martian.*"

If I hadn't worked so hard on the invite I would've thrown it at him. It was easy to see that the grey cardstock and transparent vellum wouldn't have held up against Taylor's big head. I decided to ignore him instead.

"So, girls," I said pointedly, "is there anything I need to change? Any glaring mistakes?"

"Nope. It's awesome," Madison said. "I've got volleyball practice until 4:00, but I can come over after if you need some help making the rest."

"That would be great."

"Yeah! Since its Friday we don't have orchestra rehearsal today, so I'm free to help right after school. We could make a party out of it if you want," Alyssa put in.

"Cool, I could totally use the help."

"Don't you have a hot date with Collin Farnsworth?" Taylor asked.

"No, I don't have a date with him," I grumbled. "I haven't had a date with him since last month when you saw us."

Taylor frowned. "Oops. I thought he would've been smart enough to ask you out again."

I could have smacked him. "For your information I'm seeing someone." I smiled smugly.

"Well, obviously you're not seeing him tonight."

Why does Taylor make me want to resort to violence? "No, but he will most likely call me, which is just as good." I turned to face Taylor. "Some guys work for a living, you know. They can't spend every night on the town."

"Oh . . . *oh.* So that's why I'm not invited to your party, because I spend too much time on the town? Or wait! Is it because you think I don't have a job?"

What? Where did that *come from?* I glanced at Madison and Alyssa, who both attempted to ignore us as they worked on their new charcoal-pencil assignments. Completely caught off guard, I took a moment to gather my thoughts and my art supplies before I answered Taylor.

Is he really jealous we're not asking him to the party? I thought. *If I didn't know better, I'd say he sounded a tad hurt. That can't be true. When has he ever wanted to hang out with us?*

I looked over at Taylor. I guess he had decided to work on his project, too. The tense aura around him as he gathered his supplies proved he was still agitated and wanted an answer. But I didn't know how to approach the subject.

"Taylor?" I said hesitantly.

"Yeah?" He stopped long enough to glance at me before he picked up his charcoal pencil and began to fill in the ears of a cat he had drawn yesterday.

Okay, so apparently this wasn't going to be that easy. I tried again. "You're not serious, are you?"

"About what?" Taylor answered without looking up.

Sheez. "About wanting an invite."

"I didn't say that. I just think it's a little rude is all, talking about a big party that I'm not invited to, right in front of me." His eyes narrowed a bit. "So what's the deal? Is there a reason you never include me or my friends?"

"Are you kidding me? Are you seriously saying you would *want* to come?"

"Why would you think I wouldn't?" Taylor asked.

I tried to regain my composure and defend myself. There was no way he was leaving me speechless. "The whole reason we started these parties in the first place was because you and your friends never invited us to any of your parties. So why would we think you'd want to hang out with us? It's not like you would feel comfortable anyway."

"What does that mean?"

"Taylor, honestly, think about it. You and your friends at our party? They would freak out. Seriously. Not one of your friends would want to hang out with us."

"What is up with you? Are you saying I'm a snob or something?"

"Taylor, this is a costume party. People are coming dressed up like something. This isn't just a party where people hang out and drink and stuff."

"I know. That's what makes it sound so random and cool."

"Maybe you don't understand. If someone shows up not dressed in a costume they are shown the door, as in booted out of the party. This isn't just like a thrown-together thing. We plan for months deciding on a theme and making the decorations. We spend money on this. The last thing we want is to invite someone that will make our guests feel uncomfortable."

Taylor looked hurt. "You think I'm that guy? The one that'll make everyone else uncomfortable?"

"No. I don't." I tried to smile. "You're fine, Taylor. I mean everybody likes you. Seriously. But you're asking us to include you and your friends. You definitely haven't thought this through."

"Sure I have," he replied. "I've thought about it for three years."

Why is this so hard for him to comprehend? "Let me try again." I took a deep breath. "Kylie. You honestly think Kylie Russell would be happy dressing up and attending a party we have put together?"

"Yes." He looked me right in the eyes.

"Really?" I stared back until he gave in.

"Okay. So probably not. But why wouldn't you ask us—at least give us the opportunity to go?"

"So I can waste a perfectly good invitation? I think not."

"I had no idea you were so judgmental. What gives?"

"Me, judgmental? Taylor, what gives with you? Why harp on this? You don't really want to come to a party I'm hosting. You don't want to hang out with me, or be my friend. You would die of boredom within the first ten minutes. What is up with you? Why are you so intent on—on driving me nuts? Stop worrying about stuff you don't even really care about, please."

"You don't know what I care about. You can't just make an assumption like that. You don't even know me."

"Taylor, yes, I do. I know exactly who you are and who you choose to hang with. All I have to do is look at your long list of girlfriends. Every one of them is like a cookie-cutter mold."

"They are not!" he said angrily.

"Oh no?" I grinned, glad I was able to get under his skin. "Let's ask someone, shall we? Who would know you better than anyone else in this room?" My eyes settled on Zack's sister, Emmalee Bradford. *Perfect.* "Emma," I called. Madison and Alyssa both looked up, obviously shocked at my nerve.

"Why are you doing this?" Taylor was clearly upset.

"To prove a point. Watch." I smirked as Emma practically ran over to our table.

"Yes?" she said, smiling right at Taylor.

"Taylor and I were having a little discussion, and we need your expertise."

"Really?" She giggled and flipped her hair.

"Well, since I figure you know Taylor more than anyone else in this room, due to the fact that he has spent so much time at your house, could you please list the qualities he looks for in a girl?"

ELEVEN

♥

PERFECT GIRLFRIEND

"Oh my gosh. Are you serious?" Emma wrenched her eyes away from Taylor. "Like, that is so easy!"

"Emma, you don't have to if you don't want to," Taylor said.

Taylor is so naive if he seriously thinks Emma would throw away a chance at getting his attention all to herself.

Emma giggled again. "Don't worry, I want to. Besides, you're forgetting I'm the one who wrote it down for you guys last summer, remember?"

I thought Taylor had seen a ghost, his face was so white. Apparently, he *did* remember.

"You actually made a list of qualities Taylor wants in a girl?" I asked sweetly. *She probably has the thing memorized.*

"Yeah. I wrote a separate list down for Taylor and Zack."

Alyssa raised her head at the mention of Zack.

"They each wanted a legible list of the qualities of their perfect girl," Emma went on, "so that way they could—"

"Emma!" Taylor bellowed. "Don't worry. No one needs to know why we wanted them. We're good."

"Oh?" Emma frowned at Taylor. "Did I say something wrong?"

"No, no," I reassured her. "He's just been a little on edge." The look I gave Taylor dared him to contradict me. I was surprised at the intent stare he gave me in return, almost like a challenge. *What is he trying to say? Am I wrong about him? Will what Emma says surprise me?* I pulled my eyes away from his and smiled at Emma. "Go ahead. We're ready." Madison and Alyssa were all ears.

Emma turned back to Taylor. "Your list said your perfect girl had to be funny." She began to tick off the list on her fingers. "She had to be smart. She had to be beautiful. She had to have long hair. She had to be adventurous. She had to be talented. She had to be athletic. She had to—"

Good grief!

"Okay, Emma," interrupted Taylor, "you can stop now."

"Don't be silly, Taylor." She giggled. "There's more! She had to be talkative. She had to like children. She had to be independent. She had to be trustworthy. She had to—"

What kind of a guy has a list like that for one girl? Talk about pressure. I couldn't bear to hear the rest of the list. "Whoa! Okay, Emma. We get the idea. Apparently Taylor's idea of the perfect girl is an imaginary one."

Taylor looked amused. "Are you saying there's not a girl out there with all those qualities?"

"If there is I've never met her," I responded, looking at Maddi and Alyssa. "Have you?" I asked them. Both shook their heads.

"You've never met a girl like that—" Emma imitated my sweet smile "—because you don't hang out with the people we do. Right, Taylor?"

I turned toward Emma, my mouth hanging open. *Uh, ouch. Wow. Why did she say that? Oh my gosh! Of course—she thinks she fits the list. She probably does fit it! I wonder if Taylor has noticed.*

I decided to be nice to Emma. "So have any of your girlfriends been this ideal girl?" I asked Taylor.

"No," he answered matter-of-factly.

I looked at Emma, who was smiling down at Taylor, then asked him, "And have you met a girl who you think fits that description?" I could see Emma actually hold her breath as she waited for his response. *Silly girl.*

"I—uh," he started. When he didn't say more, I turned back toward him. My eyes were captured once again by the energy in his.

What? What are you trying to say to me?

"I—uh," he tried again. His gaze settled on his hands. "I—I may have." He looked at me again. "I mean, I think so. I don't know."

Emma's breath released in an audible *whoosh* above my head, reminding me of her presence—and more importantly, her desire to capture Taylor's heart.

"You know what I think?" I grinned at Taylor as I tried to shake off the odd feeling of unease that had come over me. "I think you have met her."

"You—you do?" he asked, his eyes wide. He bit his lip, turned, and stared numbly at his drawing.

My smile began to crack. He was taking this way too seriously. "Ye–ah. I think she's someone closer than you kno–ow," I chanted lightly to catch his attention again. It worked. He glanced up, and as I looked in his eyes, the meaning there almost took my breath away. Entranced, I stared a moment before recalling where I was and that Emma was beside me. Taylor's smile began to grow and light up his whole face. I tore my eyes from his to glance at Emma and signal she was the girl I had talked of. When I looked back at him, the smile was gone. In fact, his face was completely bereft of emotion. Absolutely blank.

"Emma, what are you doing over there?" Ms. Bailey interrupted.

"I, uh . . ." Emma looked around nervously.

"She was helping me, Ms. Bailey," I answered, smiling at Emma.

"Okay. Go sit back down, Emma," Ms. B. ordered. "The next time you have a problem, Chloe, I would be glad to help you."

"Thanks," I said sheepishly. For a brief moment I paused as I picked up my charcoal pencil. I turned my head a little and perused Taylor's dark hair as he bent over his picture. *What can he be thinking?* I followed his shoulder and arm down to the paper he was working on. *Cats. He is drawing cats. What guy chooses cats for his subject in art class? That is so weird. Lions or tigers I could understand, but cats?* I couldn't help myself. I had to ask.

"Taylor, why are you drawing cats?"

"They're not cats, they're kittens," he answered without looking up.

Kittens? I tried to hide my smile but gave up. "Kittens? You? You are drawing kittens?" I attempted to smother a chuckle.

He looked up at me, grinning mischievously. "What? Didn't you know I liked furry little kittens?" At my answering snort, he said, "They're for Georgia. She loves kittens."

"Georgia who? Is she the next Kylie?"

Taylor laughed and shook his head. "You're interested in my love life? I never would have thought it, Chloe."

I rolled my eyes. "Please. Being curious at how quickly you exchange your girlfriends does not mean I'm interested."

Taylor nodded his head, accepting the hit. "Georgia is my four-year-old sister. She loves kittens. This is for her." Then he bent his head down to work on his picture again.

He has a little sister? One that he loves enough to draw pictures for? I tried to visualize Taylor with a little sister, and it was a harder thought to process than I'd imagined. I glanced across the table. Madison looked up and our eyes met. She wiggled her eyebrows and gave a quick look at Taylor before watching me roll my eyes in return.

It wasn't until much later at my house that I even thought of Taylor again. Madison, Alyssa, and I were sitting on the floor of my bedroom, attempting to make all fifty invitations in one night. That's when the ever-vigilant Madison pointed out that Taylor had looked really weird when I had motioned toward Emma earlier.

"Yeah, he did, didn't he?"

"What do you think he meant by that face?" Alyssa asked as she created more antennas. "He was so happy one second and then the next it was like someone had slapped him."

"I don't know." I shrugged as I glued a piece of typed vellum to a piece of black cardstock. "Maybe he—"

"Maybe he was hoping the girl you were talking about was a little closer to him than Emma was," Madison interrupted.

Alyssa laughed. "Who was closer than Emma? She was practically on our table."

Madison rolled her eyes. "Come on, I'm talking about someone whose knees and elbows could've touched him, she was so close." She zeroed in on me.

Dang! "No way." I tried to laugh it off. "No, he just doesn't like Emma and was freaking out about it, that's all. He wasn't hoping I was talking about myself, so stop thinking it." I pointed my finger and the miniature TV right at Madison. "I mean you.

Knock off this—this forever attempt to convince me that Taylor likes me. I can't take it." I took a deep breath. "Okay, Alyssa, tell us what you've decided to wear tomorrow when Zack takes you to the orchestra."

She smiled. "I still can't believe he bought those tickets. I've wanted to go since I first heard they were on tour."

"I have to say, Zack Bradford has definitely amazed me," Madison said.

"He really is the nicest guy," I admitted. "I wonder how I ever took his shyness as being stuck up. I'm so glad you're seeing him so you could prove me wrong."

"How many dates have you been on now?" Madison asked.

Alyssa leaned dreamily against my bed, imitation antennas now forgotten. "Five."

"Five? Really?" I asked. "I thought it was like three or something."

"Nope, five." She sighed. "Plus, I still see him every Sunday, too. But I don't count those. I just wished I knew if he liked me or not. I mean he hasn't asked me to go with him, you know?"

Madison laughed as I leaned over and tugged the hem of Alyssa's pants. "Hello? A high school guy doesn't buy way expensive tickets to an orchestra concert if he doesn't like the girl he's taking. Besides, you are so beautiful. Mark my words. I would be very surprised if he doesn't declare how much he's fallen in love with you by the end of the month."

"Besides, you can totally tell how much a guy likes you by his kiss." Madison tilted her head and stared at Alyssa.

"Ugh!" Alyssa sat up. "Don't even bring up kissing."

"Why?" Madison asked.

"Because, thanks to Tanner spying on us, we've been on five dates and Zack has been too weirded out by him to even try to kiss me goodnight." She moaned and fell back against the bed. "It's so embarrassing."

I could just imagine Alyssa's little brother peeking out the curtains at them. "Have you asked your mom and dad to keep him away?"

"Er, okay. How well do you think that will go over? 'Mom, Dad, do you mind keeping Tanner away from the window so Zack and I can make out?'"

We all laughed.

Madison shrugged. "Hey, it's worth a try."

"You at least have to ask," I said. "It's like, against the laws of dating if you don't."

Alyssa looked right at me. "All right, Chloe, I will ask my parents to help me with Tanner if you promise to ask Taylor to our party." She raised her eyebrows in a defiant challenge.

"What?" I gasped.

Madison laughed. "Look at her face! She is totally scared." She pointed her finger right at me.

Alyssa began to laugh too. I guess I looked more scared than I realized. Truth be told, I *was* scared. I was more than scared—I was terrified.

"How is this fair?" I asked. "Kissing Zack and asking Taylor to our party are two very different things."

"So. That's irrelevant," Madison said. "At least it will show Taylor that we don't consider him a snob."

"Can you believe for the last three years he has wanted to come?" Alyssa asked. "I mean, it was just so crazy when he admitted that."

"Oh, yeah," I responded sarcastically. "Thanks for jumping in there, girls. Nothing like fighting a losing battle with Taylor all on my own."

Madison laughed. "No way am I going to interrupt anything you and Taylor talk about. It's too good to miss. You really should take a step back and see the sparks that fly off the two of you."

"She's right," Alyssa remarked. "I'm always afraid I'll interrupt something and stop the flow coming from you guys. It's too exciting. I never know what you're going to say next. Honestly, I think you baffle him, the way you're always challenging him."

Madison laughed again. "You do realize you're probably the first girl in history to argue with him."

"If that's true, then he deserves it," I muttered.

"Besides," Alyssa continued, "he wanted to know why *you* hadn't invited him, not why *we* hadn't invited him. So it's only fair that you do it."

"Come on. This is way harsh. I can't beg Taylor to come to our party."

Madison grinned. "What's the big deal, Chloe?"

"I'm totally afraid he'll get the wrong idea."

"I've got it," Alyssa exclaimed dramatically as she smiled at us both. "Ask Blake too. Then Taylor can't think you like him, because you'll be around Blake all the time."

"That's perfect," I replied. "Why didn't I think of it?"

"Then we could actually meet this hunk in the flesh," Madison said.

"All right." I smiled at Alyssa. Now it was *my* turn to feel smug. "You're on. I'll invite Taylor. Just remember you have to ask your mom and dad to give you some privacy. I wanna hear about Zack's kiss."

TWELVE
♥
IT'S PARTY TIME!

"Here," I said as dropped the party invite in front of Taylor. Then I removed my backpack and sat it next to my chair. It was still a few minutes before the bell.

"What's this?" he asked as he looked up at me. He picked up the invite and flipped it over in his hand.

As if he doesn't know. "Your invite. You said you wanted one. There it is." I walked away to get my art supplies. When I came back he was waiting for me.

"So, I, uh, actually got a coveted invite?"

"It appears so, doesn't it?" I grinned so my words wouldn't sting as I plopped into my seat. "Zack got one, too."

"Why the sudden change of heart, Chloe Hart?" He grinned back at me.

"Oh, I thought it would be good for you."

He frowned slightly. "Good for me? What do you mean?"

"I thought you'd like to meet Blake." I stood up to sharpen my already-sharp pencil. For some reason I wanted to be as far away from Taylor as possible. "Be sure to bring Kylie," I called back as I walked across the room to the pencil sharpener.

As I began to sharpen my pencil to make my ploy look good, I was surprised to hear Taylor's voice behind me.

"Why are you sharpening something that's already sharp?"

Dang! "One can never be too prepared." I cranked the wheel of the sharpener. "What are you doing here?" I tossed over my shoulder.

"Oh, just sharpening my pencil. Same as you." He stepped forward and stood right behind me. His arm reached around mine to show his pencil.

I paused to compose my senses. Taylor was so close I could smell his aftershave. *He smells so good.* The tingling warmth of his arm as it touched mine nearly undid me. I turned my head slightly to look at his pencil, but I couldn't focus enough to comprehend what I was seeing. He breathed on my neck, sending a multitude of sparks racing down my back. *What is wrong with me?*

"Your hair smells good, Chloe," he whispered near my ear.

"Uh!" Instantly, I became a flurry of motion again as I realized I had nearly gone dizzy over the guy. Taylor dropped his arm and chuckled as he stepped back.

"You're not going to have much pencil left if you keep that up," he pointed out.

I pulled my sharp pencil out and saw it was couple inches shorter than when I'd started. In my haste to move away, I accidentally broke the pencil point against the sharpener. Taylor laughed.

I resigned myself to stay there long enough to sharpen the pencil again.

"Who is Blake?" Taylor asked, still a little too close for my comfort.

"The guy I'm seeing," I answered. "He's really great. You'll love him."

"I hope not," he stated. "That would be awkward."

I rolled my eyes and focused on the pencil sharpener again.

"Blake? What's his last name?"

"Winter." I sighed, trying to annoy him.

"Blake Winter," Taylor repeated. "You sure about that?"

"Yeah. Why?"

"Winter. Why does that name sound so familiar?"

I thought of how Blake worked for Taylor's dad. For some reason I didn't want to remind Taylor of that fact. "You're a smart guy, figure it out," I said as I miraculously managed to move myself and my pencil away from him. I could hear his laughter behind me as I walked away. I looked down and saw my pencil was half the size it had been when I'd started. *Why is it he always gets the last laugh?*

It was two weeks later and the Halloween party was in full swing. Almost forty vintage TV characters had arrived. Everyone looked so cool. I had dressed up like Lucille Ball from the *I Love Lucy* show. I thought with my red hair it would be the best bet.

Alyssa dressed up as Catwoman. Her costume looked really good, and Zack couldn't stop staring at her. I was so happy he had come. His costume was probably one of the coolest. He came as Cosmo Kramer from *Seinfeld,* with a brown frizzy wig and all. He did a mean impression of Kramer, too. We were all impressed.

Madison went all Scooby Doo on us and dressed as Daphne. She had found this funky purple dress from the thrift store. It looked so cute. With her red wig and lime green scarf, I almost didn't recognize her.

I couldn't wait to see Blake. He was supposed to come as Bo Duke from *The Dukes of Hazzard*. As soon as I'd told him about the vintage TV show theme, he'd announced his character. With his blond hair and those dimples, I knew he would make a killer Bo. I just hoped he showed up before Taylor did. As of today, Taylor had insisted he would bring Kylie to the party. I kind of thought he would change his mind at the last moment. *He still could. Now, that would be a relief.*

The doorbell rang and I ran to answer it. *Please let this be Blake.*

"Hello. Come on in." I smiled to hide my disappointment as I let Knight Rider and Batman in. They were both guys I knew from four-wheeling. Just like a proper hostess, I exclaimed over their costumes and pointed them to the back room. Before I shut the door I searched again for Blake's truck. *Where is he?*

"Chloe!"

I turned to see Alyssa hurry through the crowd. "What's up?"

She stopped in front of me and looked around, then pulled me down the side hall and into my bedroom.

I frowned. "What?"

She gulped dramatically. "Ethan just told me that Blake's not coming."

"What? Why? Did something happen? Is he okay?"

"Apparently—" I had to lean over to catch her words "—Blake isn't coming because of Taylor."

"Taylor? What? Why? That's crazy. What has Taylor got to do with anything?"

"Ethan said that Taylor stormed up to the front desk of the hotel where Blake was working and demanded that he tell him his name. As soon as Blake said, 'Blake Winter,' Taylor turned and stomped into his father's office and told him to fire Blake."

My jaw dropped. "Taylor wouldn't dare! What gives him the right to do that?"

"Yeah, I guess Mr. Anderson talked to Blake for over an hour after Taylor left," Alyssa continued. "Anyway, Blake found out Taylor was coming to the party and opted to work tonight to avoid him."

All of a sudden I felt sick to my stomach. *Poor Blake.*

"I just can't believe Taylor would ever do that. It's so weird," Alyssa said. "Maybe Ethan heard wrong."

"I doubt that. I can very well believe Taylor did just what Ethan said." I was fuming. "He was totally hounding me a week ago, wanting to know who Blake was. If Taylor wants to bug me, then fine. But to hurt Blake? No way. Taylor Anderson has just crossed the line." *It infuriates me the way popular guys think they can run everything! Just because he's king of the school doesn't mean Taylor needs to get into everybody's business.*

Right then the doorbell rang. I half smiled at Alyssa and walked out of my room toward the front door. As I stepped back into the party zone, I almost wanted to cancel the whole thing. I had looked forward to seeing Blake, and now he wasn't even coming. Because of Taylor.

I opened the door and almost slammed it in Taylor's face. *The nerve.* On second thought I figured if I did that, it would show Taylor how mad he had made me. I didn't want to give him the satisfaction of seeing how much he could affect me. I opened the door wider and pasted a smile on my face.

"Welcome." My voice nearly cracked from the strain. "Wow, Kylie. You make a beautiful Jeannie." I muffled a smirk at her no-brainer costume from the *I Dream of Jeannie* show. How many cheerleaders would've worn that exact same costume? Maybe it was a good thing I only had one coming to the party, or my house would've been be full of Barbara Eden wannabes.

"Thanks," Kylie replied. Her beauty-pageant smile glowed as she passed me and entered the house. One look at her face spoke volumes. She was not happy to be around me and my "little" friends.

Good. Maybe she'll hate the party so much she'll convince Taylor to leave early.

"What do you think of my costume?" he asked as he brushed past me.

I tried to focus on his outfit but couldn't. Still silently seething, I found the longer I stood in his company the angrier I became.

"It's great," I mumbled.

As I shut the front door, I took a deep breath and willed myself to remain calm. I knew it would be really bad if I made a scene in front of everyone. Even though I wanted a whole lot of questions answered, I knew now was not the time.

You know, it's a real good thing I didn't fall for the guy like everyone else, I thought. *I knew something like this would happen.* Actually that wasn't true. I didn't know Taylor was *that* mean. What was with him? Seriously, what guy would maliciously try to get someone else fired? Especially since he knew I liked Blake. That's what bothered me the most. He had no right to act the way he did, but it was like he was trying to purposely hurt me and Blake.

"Hey, Chloe, are you all right?" I turned to my right to find Taylor standing next to me.

"Oh, it's you." I went to brush past him and find Madison or Alyssa to man the door. I wasn't feeling very hostess-y at the moment, and I needed a few minutes to myself to shake this mood. But Taylor was faster than I was and grabbed my arm before I could escape.

"Chloe, wait. What's wrong?" He genuinely looked concerned.

How could a guy this intuitive not realize the last thing I wanted was to be next to him? "I'm not feeling that great," I answered. Pointedly, I looked down at his hand on my arm. "Do you mind?"

"Sorry." Taylor released me like he had been scorched.

"Excuse me," I muttered as I walked away. I found Madison in the kitchen with a group of our friends. She seemed to be having a great time. The noise from the family room was happy and a bit boisterous. My mom was in there telling jokes with Alyssa and Zack until the rest of the guests arrived and the real games began.

"Hey, Chloe—er, I mean Lucy!" Madison called. "You've got to hear this idea." She broke away from the group and moved toward me. I stopped and waited for her as she carved a path through six or seven people who were in line for the food. She was all smiles once she reached me, but after a quick look at my face she blurted, "What's up? Is everything all right?"

"I'm not feeling too good. Would you mind watching the door for me while I sit out for a few minutes?" I asked.

"Sure." I knew she wanted to ask more.

"Thanks," I replied. "Just give me about ten minutes, okay?"

"No problem." She looked at me curiously but didn't say anything.

Without a backward glance, I escaped to my bedroom. With the door shut behind me I paced for a minute and then stopped. I really wanted to scream or something, but I was so afraid someone would hear me. The laughter and joviality of the party crept in my subconscious. *At least they're all having fun. Ugh! Taylor!* I began to pace again, this time with no clear thought or direction as I fumed.

I knew it. I knew all popular guys were the same. Taylor is such a moron. Seriously. Why would he do such a thing? Why would he march into the hotel and demand Blake be fired? It just doesn't make sense. What has Blake ever done to him?

I jumped at the sound of a knock on my door. I couldn't believe it had been ten minutes already. Quickly, I picked up the teddy bear on my bed and sat down.

"Come in." I called, then waited for Madison to open the door.

"Is it safe?" Taylor asked as he peeked his head into my room.

THIRTEEN
♥
CONFUSING CONFESSIONS

"You?" I was so astonished that I chucked the stuffed bear right at Taylor. Instantly, he disappeared. As the door closed, I watched my favorite bear smack it right where Taylor's head had been. The bear landed in a heap on my bedroom floor. I could hear Taylor chuckle on the other side of the door.

"What do you want?" I marched over to save my bear.

"I want to know if it's safe to come in," Taylor replied.

"Uh, that would be a no," I answered through the door.

"Why?"

"Well, first off, you may lose your head if you come through that door right now. Secondly, my dad would hogtie you quicker than you could say 'help' if he knew you were in my room."

Taylor laughed.

"I wasn't kidding," I warned through the door.

"I'm sure you weren't." I could hear the smile in his voice. "I can still think it's funny, can't I?"

"No."

"Okay, look. I'm standing outside of your room during the middle of a party, ignoring my girlfriend, just so I can hear you sulk. I think I'm on the losing end here."

"Of all the—" I yanked open the door and glared at Taylor. "I do not sulk!"

He had one arm leaned against the doorframe while the rest of him filled the doorway. He grinned. "I knew that would get you to open the door."

"Oh!" I tried to shut the door once again, but he was quicker than me. His right foot blocked the entrance, and the door wouldn't even budge.

"What are you mad about?" he asked calmly.

"Nothing. Now move." I pushed against his chest to get him to shift enough so I could close the door. It didn't work. I shoved harder.

"Chloe." His voice above my head caused me to look up at him. "Don't do that."

"Why?"

"I don't think it's a good idea for you to touch me." His blue eyes glittered.

I looked down at my hands and saw them splayed against Taylor's chest. They moved up and down slightly with the rhythm of his breathing. Instantly, I removed my hands and placed them on my hips.

"Well, then move already," I said defensively, refusing to acknowledge the awkward situation.

"I'm not moving until you tell me what's bothering you. Besides, this is your party, the party you have been waiting for all year. Something has upset you. What is it?"

"Look, I'm really disappointed right now, and I don't want to talk about it, okay? If I bring it up, I'll harp on it the rest of the night and then possibly ruin this party for everyone else. If you don't mind, I'd rather talk about something different."

"What would you like to talk about, then?" Taylor asked as if standing outside my bedroom door while we chatted was a normal occurrence.

Nothing. I want you to leave. I mean, why is he here anyway? I don't get it. Would the back-stabbing Taylor really come to my room and check on me? It doesn't make sense.

"What?" He chuckled. "Why do you have the look on your face?"

"I'm trying to figure you out. I hear so many different things about you. The problem is, they totally contradict each other."

"Well, as I've said before, people like to talk about me," he smiled ruefully. "I wouldn't believe all you hear."

"No matter who I've heard it from?" I asked.

"Well, if it's from me, then you're okay." He grinned arrogantly.

I found I was more contemplative than angry, so in a way I was grateful Taylor had sought me out. It did help to ease my mood.

"Chloe," Madison called as she walked down the hall. "The party's ready to begin. Are you—oh!" She stopped as she turned the corner and saw Taylor and I having our little "heart to Hart."

"Yeah, I'm ready. Thanks." I smiled at her.

Her eyes were so huge it was almost comical. The look she sent warned me I better tell her everything later.

Taylor wasn't even phased as he smiled and asked Madison how she was doing. He even commented on her Daphne outfit as we walked back up the hallway. I opted to walk in front of them. The hallway just wasn't built wide enough for three people. Of course, I was more flabbergasted than anything when I overheard Madison ask about Taylor's mustache.

Mustache? I stopped and whipped around so fast I had to hold on to the wall. My action forced Madison and Taylor to stop as well. *Well, I'll be! He does have a mustache.* "You have a mustache!" I was so shocked. *Why didn't I notice it before?* "How long has that been on?"

He chuckled. "Since I left my house."

"Really?" I gasped.

"Yeah." His smile grew wide. "Do you like it?"

No. He looks like a total dork. On the other hand . . . "Yes. It suits you." I smiled back. "Who are you supposed to be, anyway?"

"Uh, you can't tell?" Taylor looked surprised.

I looked at Madison to see if she knew. She shrugged her shoulders. "I don't know."

"Come on, at least try." Taylor turned so Madison could see all of him. She chewed on her lip. "Well, you kinda look like Luke Duke, except I didn't think he had a mustache." She turned to me. "Did he?"

Luke Duke? From The Dukes of Hazzard? *Are you kidding me? Taylor dressed up like Luke, while Blake was supposed to be Bo!*

"No." Taylor laughed. "I was hoping to be someone a bit more unique."

"Hey, *The Dukes of Hazzard* is unique." I defended Blake's choice. *Okay, so it's not, but it's definitely a classic.* If I was completely honest, though, it was about as original as *I Dream of Jeannie.*

"Whatever," Taylor replied. "You really can't tell who I am?"

"Nope," Madison said.

He looked at me.

"Not a clue."

"Come on! I'm Magnum PI."

"Who?" we said at the same time, staring back at him.

"You know, Tom Selleck. Blue eyes. Black hair. Mustache. Ring a bell?"

"Sorry. That must be a guy show," Madison said. "That's okay, though. You dressed up and that counts for something. Not to mention you went out on a limb with that mustache." She giggled.

I turned around and started to head toward the family room in the back of the house. *Taylor's mustache. I still can't believe I didn't see that thing. I guess it just proves what my mental state is like at the moment.*

My mom and most of the guests were waiting for me when I got to the family room. She had everyone sit on folding chairs in a huge circle around the area. Dad had moved our couches to the garage to make space for the fifty chairs. I never thought all those chairs would fit, but miraculously they did.

"All right," Mom said over the hum of the crowd. "Who's ready for a game?"

She had planned to hang out with Dad, Cass, and Claire tonight at the diner and a double-feature movie. But instead I asked her to host the games for me. My mom knows a load of crazy games. Some of them I'm positive she made up. My friends love her, though, and once word got out that my mom was planning the games, everybody began to speculate just what she'd have them do. If I didn't know better, I'd swear the party attendance was as good as it was because everyone knew she'd be there helping.

"Okay, guys, are you ready?" she asked in her best circus-director voice. "The first vintage TV character we're going to honor with a game is Porky Pig. Get your snouts ready, because our game is called Oink, Piggy, Oink!"

I began to laugh and attempt to snort with the rest of the group as I found an empty chair. Yep. This was definitely going to be a night to remember. *I just wish Blake was here to share it with me.*

{♥}

"So how was the party?" Blake's deep voice in the receiver tickled my ear. I was on my bed sitting cross-legged as I flipped through a magazine. It was Saturday afternoon. Thank goodness Blake let me sleep in before he called to get the news. The party had ended way later than I thought it would.

"It went really well, as far as the party goes. Everyone really enjoyed themselves . . ." my voice trailed off.

"But?" prompted Blake.

I grimaced. "But I tried really hard to be happy. I'm not sure it worked, though." I wondered if I should bring up what I had heard about Taylor. I didn't want Blake to be embarrassed.

"Oh, so I guess my nemesis was there, then?" he asked. "Is that why you weren't happy?"

"Your nemesis?" *Is he talking about Taylor?*

Blake snorted. "Yeah, you know, that Collin guy."

"Yes. My mom invited him." I rolled my eyes and turned the page to a really cute advert for makeup. "It was no big deal, though." *At least compared to everything else.* "Madison came to my rescue."

"What do you mean?"

"Every time Collin came near me or started to speak to me, Madison would get his attention. She totally saved me."

Blake laughed. "Are you telling me the guy actually tried to talk to you this time?"

"Yeah, apparently he tried. It was kind of weird now that I think about it."

"So who was Collin?" Blake asked as I flipped another page.

"What? Oh, you mean, who did he come as?"

"Yeah."

"He came as the Fonz. You know, from *Happy Days?*"

"Really! I'm surprised. That's not a bad costume choice."

"Well, he didn't look quite as good as Henry Winkler, and he really couldn't work the mannerisms and accent. But all in all, he wasn't too bad. I was surprised too." I decided to brave it out and bring up Taylor. "So do you know who Mangus PI is? Some guy came as him last night."

"Do you mean Magnum PI?"

"Yeah, that's it." I laughed.

"Uh, yeah," Blake answered. "That was one cool show back in the '80s."

"Really?"

"My dad owns the whole DVD collection of that series. So get this. The guy, Magnum, used to be a navy SEAL, right? Well, now he lives in Hawaii on some millionaire's property, as a private investigator, which is what PI stands for."

"Oh?" I asked, trying to feign interest. I flipped another page of the magazine.

"Yes." Blake was really getting into it. "You know the best part? The guy got to drive a Ferrari 308 GTS. I don't know what guy on the planet wouldn't want to drive one of those."

"Wow, it sounds neat," I commented.

"You have no idea. He totally lived the dream life. They just don't make shows like that anymore. So who dressed up like Magnum? Is he part of our four-wheeling group?"

"No." I hesitated. "It's—well, his name's Taylor Anderson. I don't know if you know him."

"Taylor?" The anger in Blake's voice surprised me. "It *would* be him."

"So you know him?"

"Yeah. Unfortunately, the aaa—the—the . . . what's the word you use for the A-word?"

"Oh, uh, chicken butt," I said sheepishly.

"Chicken butt?" All at once, Blake began to laugh. "You're kidding me, right?"

"Nope. Wish I were, especially right now. You have no idea." I giggled, totally embarrassed.

"I'm sorry. I can't say it." He chuckled. "I just can't."

"You already have," I pointed out. "But if it helps, I personally use the words 'stupid,' 'imbecile,' 'jerk' or 'egotistical moron' to describe Taylor."

"Really? You're kidding me. There's actually a girl alive who doesn't like my cousin? You are so lucky we're on the phone right now. Because if we weren't, I'd grab you and kiss you so hard your head would swim."

FOURTEEN

♥

DOUBLE TROUBLE

My head swam. I decided to ignore his comment about wanting to kiss me. "You're Taylor's cousin?"

"Regrettably, I have to say that is my lot in life—to play second fiddle to the pampered Taylor Anderson," Blake replied.

"You're kidding! I had no idea."

"Yeah, well, not very many people do. I try to keep it secret for as long as possible. That's why I moved here, though. Lionel Anderson's my uncle. He offered me a job. I needed one, so I came."

"But I thought Taylor was surprised to learn your name," I blurted without thinking.

"Oh, you heard about that?" Blake sighed. "Yeah, that would be Taylor, all right. He was surprised to hear my name was Blake Winter, since he calls me Blake Wilder. Wilder's my real name. I changed it because I wanted to make a new start with you guys."

"Well, for the record I like Winter. I think it's a great name."

"Thanks. Apparently Taylor doesn't. I don't get that kid. He never lets me have a moment to myself, you know? Sometimes I wonder if he's jealous his dad and I get along so well. For some reason, no matter how nice I am to him, Taylor and I have never gotten along. This isn't the first job he tried to get me fired from, either."

"No way."

"So have you always detested Taylor, or is this a new feeling?" he asked.

"Oh, always, ever since I first moved here three years ago."

"When do you turn eighteen?"

Huh? "Not till April. Why?"

Blake muttered something under his breath, then said, "You better call me the second you're eighteen, you hear?"

"Why?" A giggle escaped my throat.

"Because" —his deep voice sent exciting chills down my spine— "then you won't be jailbait."

Jailbait? "Oh." I gulped.

His sexy laugh would've caused my knees to buckle if I'd been standing. "Don't worry—I won't ravish you before then."

"He said *what?*" Taylor almost bellowed behind me.

I had whispered it to Madison and Alyssa as Taylor walked over to get his art supplies on Monday. But obviously he overheard me when he came back. My girlfriends and I had leaned in to talk over—again—what Blake had said on Saturday. It had been all we had discussed that whole weekend. The fact that Blake was Taylor's cousin was mind-boggling. But adding in the jealousy between the two was more than any girl could handle, especially when you had to face the fact that Taylor wasn't as perfect as everybody thought.

I had just finished exclaiming over the "jailbait" comment again, which was definitely the worst thing Taylor could've overheard. *Why does he always manage to unnerve me?*

Taylor dumped his art supplies on the table. He pulled out his chair and loomed over me. "Did you just say that Blake wanted to know when you were eighteen so you wouldn't be considered jailbait anymore?"

Does he have to say everything so flippin' loud? "Will you sit down?" I hissed.

"Not until you answer me." His stubborn face reminded me of a two-year-old.

I used my sweet smile. "Well, then stand. I don't care. Until you learn to treat me with some respect and courtesy, you're not getting any answers anyway. I don't care how loud you are about it. If you want to discuss your cousin at all, then I suggest you get on my good side and treat me a little nicer."

Taylor sat down. "Why do you have to get so defensive about everything?"

"Excuse me?" I turned to face him. "I was under the impression the only one having defensive issues about anything was you. I'm just here to make sure you behave like a decent human being when you voice them, because obviously you're going to voice them whether I want you to or not."

He was clearly agitated. "Okay, look. I don't know what Blake has told you. Obviously, you know we're cousins, which is more than he usually divulges. But just get off your high horse for a moment. Simmer down—"

"Taylor," I interrupted, "for a smart guy, you really know how to get on a girl's nerves. High horse? Simmer down? As if I'm upset or something?"

"—and listen to me," he finished. "Please?"

Fine. I huffed. "What?"

"No matter what you may think right now, Blake is not a good guy. Okay? Just promise me you'll stay away from him." His blue eyes pleaded into mine.

I turned away so I wouldn't be affected by them. "Thanks for caring," I said sarcastically, "but I'm a big girl and can handle myself. I'll decide when and where I'll end my relationship with Blake. If I do, that is." I turned and smiled at him.

Taylor nearly lost it. "No! I absolutely forbid you to see Blake again!" I'd never seen Taylor so upset.

"You *forbid* me?" I challenged. *The nerve.* I would've laughed except it wasn't funny. Comical, yes. Funny, no.

Any hope Taylor had to get me to listen to him was over with that rash statement, and I could tell he knew it. With one word, he had completely painted himself as the black-hearted villain I had suspected he was. There was nothing he could say that would deter me from Blake now. I was through being troubled by what Taylor thought. Just because the rest of the world danced to his tune didn't mean I was going to. I refused to even look at him again, and we spent the rest of art class in frustrated silence.

Later that evening Madison, Alyssa, and I were on a three-way call discussing the day's events, and more importantly, Taylor's odd behavior.

"Are you sure?" Alyssa asked. "It really sounded like he was upset today. I mean *worried* for you. To me it just seems that he can't be all that bad."

"What? Of course he can be that bad," I insisted. "This is Taylor Anderson we're talking about here—one of the biggest jerks in our school."

"Jerk or not, Chloe," Madison said, "Taylor is still the most popular guy around. And whether he is worried about you or not, you shouldn't turn him away like you do. Think of it. If Taylor paid as much attention to me as he pays to you, I would definitely be using that to my advantage. I would make him think I liked him."

"Are you kidding me?" I gasped.

"No, I'm not. By pushing Taylor back like you do, you are totally throwing away a chance of at least being friends with the most popular guy in school. I'm not sure it's a smart idea to throw that away. I do understand that you have different views than the rest of us when it comes to Taylor, and I have always respected that. I just think that maybe now that it's becoming more and more obvious that he may like you, you should give him some credit."

"Besides, we really don't know what to think about this whole thing," Alyssa said.

I could hardly believe I was talking to my two best friends. If I didn't know better, I'd have thought I was on the phone with Emmalee Bradford, not Madison and Alyssa. "Excuse me, but I know exactly what to think. There is really nothing else to say on this subject. Taylor has been repeatedly rude to Blake because he is jealous of him. And he doesn't like me as much as you think. He was just mad I wouldn't listen to him like everyone else does. End of discussion."

"What if Taylor is right?" Alyssa asked. "What if Blake isn't a good guy?"

"Then let Taylor prove it to me. As far as I can see, Blake is the one who is wronged. Taylor has everything he has ever wanted or needed. Besides, what reason is there for Blake to lie?"

"Well, just be careful, okay?" Alyssa sighed.

I laughed. "I'm always careful. Just think of what my parents put those poor guys through first. It takes a lot for a guy to even want to date me."

"Speaking of dates, Alyssa," Madison said. "Where are you going with Zack this Saturday?"

"Oh, he's busy, but we're planning on going out the next Saturday. I'm not sure what we'll be doing, though.

"I'm still freaking out about last Saturday's date," I put in, grateful for the change in subject. "It was so cool that he waited with you outside the cast door after the show, just so you could get autographs as the players left."

"The way you described the orchestra almost made me wish I had gone too," Madison said. "Which is surprising, considering my take on classical music."

"How did the kiss go?" I teased. "Was Tanner there?"

"Did you talk to your parents about getting rid of him?" Madison asked.

"Yes, I did. And yes, he was still there." Alyssa groaned. "My parents said they would not interfere with the natural course of things, but it was okay. During the last half of the concert, Zack leaned over and held my hand. I thought I was going to die!" She sighed wistfully.

Madison began to laugh. "You two have only just started holding hands?"

"Could there be a shyer couple in the world?" I asked Madison.

"No," she responded, "I think Alyssa and Zack get the award."

"Well, this relationship might just actually last," I said. "Think about it. By the time they're forty, Zack might propose. Of course, they won't actually get married until they're fifty."

Madison and I lost it. We both started to laugh hard.

"Hey!" Alyssa said. "We're not that bad." She began to giggle. "On second thought, maybe we are."

I glanced at the clock—9:15. "Hey, girls, I better run. I've got to start research for my English essay. I just hope Cass is off the computer now."

"You still don't have it done?" Alyssa sounded shocked.

"Isn't it due Friday?" Madison asked. "I have Mr. Young too, and mine's been done at least a week now."

"Ugh. Don't remind me," I mumbled. "Cassidy has met some guy on Facebook and has hogged the computer ever since. She drives me crazy. She better be off now or I'll drag her off if she doesn't go willingly."

"Well, I better run too," Alyssa said. "I've got trig homework." She sighed again. "Why do I put myself through this?"

"I'm homework-free today," bragged Madison. "So I think I'm going to veg in front of the TV. Dad's working late again."

"All right then, daw-lings," I said in my movie-star voice, "I will see you tomorrow"

"Bye!" chorused Alyssa and Madison just before I hung up the phone.

I wandered into the kitchen and overheard my mom on her cell phone.

"Okay, Collin. That's great, then. We'll see you Friday. Bye!" she gushed into the phone.

Oh, no! "What's going on?" I asked.

She positively glowed, she was so happy. "That was Collin just now. He says he wanted to come over for dinner on Friday night. He has a very important question to ask you." She ran over and hugged me. "Ooh! This is going to be so cute."

Are you kidding me? "Wait. Collin's coming here in four days? What does he have to ask me?"

"I guess you'll just have to wait to find out." Mom smiled.

Why me? I'm so going to die.

That would have given me enough to dread and torment myself over for the next few days, if Zack hadn't surprised us all with his announcement on Wednesday. It totally trumped anything I was feeling sorry for myself about.

FIFTEEN
❤
A NOT-SO-FLATTERING OFFER

Thank goodness no one from the school knew about Alyssa and Zack seeing each other. It wasn't surprising, I guess, since the two were never together around kids from school—other than at our party, where everyone was more surprised to see the school's reigning king and prince than to ponder why they came. I'm totally excluding Kylie, I know, but the way she pouted the whole night, it was obvious to everyone else that she wasn't happy to be there. On the other hand, Taylor and Zack got involved in every game, which completely removed any awkwardness my guests might have felt with them—the "in" guys—being there. And that turned it into—I hate to say it—probably our greatest bash to date.

Still, I don't think anyone realized Alyssa and Zack were sort of a couple, mainly because they were both so darned shy about it. They spoke to each other, but no more than they did to anyone else. All in all, I guess it was a good thing they were so quiet about their relationship. If everyone did know,

Jenni James

Alyssa would've become the biggest center of gossip at school on Wednesday afternoon. I'm not sure if she could've handled that. She had a hard enough time with it already.

"But I don't understand why," I said to her. "Did he give a reason?"

"No." Alyssa sniffed. "He just said he couldn't see me anymore. And that we . . . we had to break up." She leaned on my shoulder and burst into tears. Thankfully, the parking lot had emptied pretty fast today, and even the students that saw her meltdown had no idea of the reason for it.

"Shh." I patted her back. *I wish Madison were here. She would know just what to say to Alyssa to make her smile again.*

"But I didn't even know we were going *out* out. That's the worst part." Alyssa sobbed harder. "I had a boyfriend and didn't even know it!"

"Wow," was all I managed. I was very disappointed in Zack. I had really begun to think he was for real. *Popular guys—boys—can be such losers. Do they really have no idea how much they can crush a girl?* As much as I tried, I couldn't convince myself that they didn't know what they were doing when they broke a girl's heart.

"Let's go get some milkshakes," I suggested.

"Um, I'd rather not," Alyssa mumbled. After a few more sniffles, she released me and stood up, wiping her face with her hand.

I rummaged in my backpack and found one of those travel tissue packs. "Here." I handed Alyssa a tissue. Then, after seeing her face, I handed her another one.

She giggled. "Yeah. My mom doesn't let me buy waterproof mascara."

"I'll say." I smiled. Alyssa's face was covered in black streaks—or make that *blotches* now that she had wiped her

130

face. "Let's go to your house instead. I really don't think you're up for facing anyone in public."

"Thanks . . . I think." She giggled again. "Just give me a minute and I'll be myself."

Good ol' Alyssa. She always manages to make the best of things. She could find the positive light in a blackout. I decided right then that I would call Ethan and let him know I wasn't going to make it four-wheeling tonight. Friends come first. And Alyssa definitely needed a pick-me-up.

By Thursday we were convinced there must be something in the drinking water. It was all over campus that morning that Taylor had broken up with Kylie, too. Not that it was such a big surprise. I mean, we were talking about Taylor, right? He was bound to break up with Kylie sooner or later. I just wished the whole school wouldn't care so much when he became single again. I kind of hoped he would choose another girl quickly so we could all be put out of our misery.

As far as art went, Taylor and I were on polite speaking terms. I had decided I wouldn't let him affect me anymore, and it seemed to be working. As long as I stayed detached from whatever comment he made, we got along.

Before I knew it, it was Friday. As much as I wished it was still Wednesday or Thursday, it wasn't. I had prayed I would be sick or something so I'd have an excuse not to come out of my room. I almost convinced myself I had a headache. But Mom didn't even hesitate when she told me to "take a Tylenol and deal with it." I was making the most of my almost headache on my bed in my dark room—well, as dark as I could make it at 5:00 p.m., which honestly wasn't very dark at all.

I groaned out loud when I heard the doorbell ring and then my mom happily welcome Collin in the house.

"Chloe," Mom called in a sing-song voice, "Collin's here."

"Coming!" Disgusted, I dragged myself off the bed. To kill a bit more time, I decided to walk over to my mirror and fix my hair. Then, of course, I had to straighten my clothes. I took a couple more minutes to add jewelry, but then I changed my mind and took it off again. I didn't want to look like I was trying to impress the guy.

After Mom shouted my name a second time, I realized I couldn't get away with hiding in my room any longer, so I grudgingly made my way down the hall to the dining room. I could overhear my mom as she practically simpered to Collin, "You have to excuse Chloe. She hasn't been feeling well today. The poor dear."

I rolled my eyes as I came around the corner.

"There she is!" my mom said, clearly relieved.

Collin was all friendly smiles as I sat down next to my father and across from him. Dinner went better than I thought, thanks to Dad's sense of humor. Every time Collin acted weird or pulled out his phone, Dad looked at me and raised his eyebrows. I was so relieved to find that someone else in my family thought Collin was strange.

But dinner didn't last long enough. Before I knew it, I found myself being whisked outside to the privacy of the front yard, with Collin right behind me. I turned just in time to see my mother's blissful smile as she shut the front door behind us. In an instant I realized just how alone I was, and a feeling of dread came over me. I walked over to the little bench at the front of the house and sat down. I didn't care whether Collin followed me or not. It was like I knew exactly what he would ask before the words ever left his mouth.

"Chloe?" He stood right over me.

I rubbed the toe of my shoe against the worn spot in the lawn in front of the bench. "Yep," I answered, not looking up.

Collin cleared his throat.

Great. Here he goes. I just wanted this moment to end.

"Chloe, um, I've been thinking a lot lately about how my life needs to change."

Yeah, you think?

"And well, my mom mentioned that maybe I wouldn't spend so much time on the computer if I had a girlfriend."

Could this get any more embarrassing? I refused to look up at him. Instead I continued to study the ground.

He plowed on. "And I was thinking you would probably be the safest bet—I mean since you're nice and all, and I know you. So, so—that's it."

That's it? As in what? Does he think we're going out? Speechless, I looked up as Collin uncomfortably squatted down in front of me. He attempted to hold my hands, but I pulled them away.

He cleared his throat again. "I guess all we have left to do is seal the deal." He started to lean in close with his lips puckered.

Ahh! Instantly I jumped up. I knocked into Collin in the process, which caused him to lose his balance and topple backward.

Oh my gosh! Oh my gosh! Oh my gosh! I began to panic. I turned my back from him while he scrambled to his feet. *What am I going to say? Be nice. Firm, but nice.*

"Collin." I turned around to face his naive smile. "Look, I really think you're a nice guy. But I'm—I don't think it'll work out, but thanks for asking."

Collin just kept grinning at me, then laughed awkwardly.

"Collin, I'm serious."

Something must've clicked in his brain, because he suddenly frowned. "But I don't understand. Are you going out with someone already?"

"Well, no."

"Well, then, don't you need a boyfriend?"

Are you for real? "No, Collin, I don't *need* a boyfriend. I'm perfectly fine on my own, thank you."

"But your mother said you would say yes if I asked. She told my mom—I don't understand . . ."

I lost it. "You know what? I don't have to listen to this." I walked back in the house and slammed the door behind me, leaving Collin outside. I know it was a bit harsh, but I was so sick of people bossing me around.

To say my mom was mad would be an understatement. She was positively livid, which was fine with me, because I didn't care what she thought anymore. I let her run outside and comfort a sullen Collin while I ran to my room and slammed that door, too.

After a few minutes of pacing up and down I heard a knock. "Go away!"

"Chloe?" It was my dad.

Oh, great. "Yeah, you can come in." I grabbed my bear and plopped on the bed.

My dad walked into my room and pulled out the desk chair. Straddling it backwards, he sat down and faced me. The look on his face made me feel awful. I didn't even know what to say to him.

"Chloe, I'm not worried about Collin, if that's what's bothering you," he stated. "I'm sure someone as oblivious as that kid will easily forgive and forget. I'm worried about you and your relationship with your family."

"Oh?"

"This isn't like you. Snapping at people, taking things so seriously. The Chloe I know would have found tonight utterly hilarious and found a way to let that poor boy down gently."

Not sure what to say, I remained silent.

"What's going on with you?" my dad asked. "Is it anything you want to talk about?"

"Not really. I don't know what's wrong."

He ran his hand through his faded blond hair. "Look. Your mom is pretty adamant that you become Collin's girlfriend, even if it's just for a few weeks. She thinks you are being very stubborn, selfish, and prideful. In fact, she asked me to come in and talk to you."

"She did?"

"Yes. And you have to admit she's got a point. Now here's the problem," Dad continued. "She wants you grounded if you don't accept Collin."

I grimaced. *They can't force me to be the guy's girlfriend, can they?*

"And I will ground you if you do," Dad finished.

Mom's vengeful "No!" could be heard just outside my door as I realized what my father had said.

What? "Thank you!" I ran across the room and hugged him so tight I almost knocked him over. "I love you." He hugged me back. "And don't worry. It's nothing, Dad. I'm fine."

"Is there anything I can do?" he asked.

I thought for a moment, then smiled. "Just please don't make me deal with Mom."

SIXTEEN

♥

ONE WORD: MORP

By the middle of November, I had begun to wonder if Blake had been drinking the same water as Taylor and Zack. Not that Blake and I were an official item or anything—definitely nothing of the sort. It's just when you get used to a guy calling you almost every day it becomes pretty noticeable when he stops. So by the time December rolled around and Ethan announced that Blake had a girlfriend, I wasn't too surprised. It had been almost four weeks since I had last heard from him. His new schedule at the hotel didn't leave room for Wednesday-night four-wheeling, either. But that was okay. With Madison, Alyssa, and I so busy with our own schedules it was nice to have the odd weekend free to hang out like old times. Besides, December was a time to plan for holiday events, parties, and, of course, morp.

Honestly, is there a person alive who doesn't love morp? It was only our school's biggest dance other than prom. As funny as it sounds, morp is "prom" spelled backwards, and therefore that was the theme of the night. For Backwards Night, the girls did everything: the tickets, the dinner, the photos, the ride—everything. We even got to choose the matching outfits that were worn that night. Thank goodness the dance was a casual one.

I found out our school held morp in January so all of the proceeds could go toward prom in April. Traditionally, the guy a girl asks to morp is the guy she is secretly hoping will ask her to prom. So imagine my complete and utter surprise when a desperate Taylor barged into art class one Friday and asked me to help him find a girl to take him to morp.

"I need help," he said desperately. "Will you help me get a date to morp, please?"

His eyes were almost aquamarine today. *Why is it guys usually have the prettiest eyes?* I tried to make sense of what I had heard. "Let me get this straight. You need someone to ask you to morp?"

"Yes, immediately! Will you help me?"

You need help finding a date to morp? You? "But why?"

Taylor sat in the chair next to me. "Because of Sydney Ellis."

"Sydney?" She was probably one of the rudest cheerleaders I had ever known. Where Kylie would at least fake like she liked you, Sydney was your typical movie "mean girl." "What about her?" I asked.

Taylor collapsed forward on the table and buried his face in his hands. "She's just asked me to morp. I don't know what to do. I haven't answered her yet, thanks to her perfect timing. She asked right as the bell rang. But I'll see her next hour and she'll be expecting my answer then. I need someone else to ask me now, so I can tell her that I'm already taken. I really don't want to go with her."

No, you really don't. "Let me make sure I understand. You, Taylor Anderson, need help finding a date ASAP to morp, correct?"

"Isn't that what I just said?"

"Yes, but it's so unexpected I wanted to make sure I heard you correctly."

"So you can help?"

"Well, yeah. I can help you find someone. Now let's see, there's a whole room full of girls. Just choose one. Anyone."

"Really?" Taylor sat up.

"Yes, really. As a matter of fact, I could get any girl in the school to take you. Who would you love to go with more than anyone else? I'll ask her. Then, bingo, she's yours."

"I don't think she wants to go with me."

I rolled my eyes as I stood up. "Please, Taylor." Then it hit me just as I was about to walk away to get my art supplies ready. "Oh! You mean Kylie?"

"What? Kylie? No." He pushed himself up and followed me over to the shelves.

"Oh?" I shrugged. "So who is she?" I reached up and pulled out Taylor's scratchboard, then my own.

He walked over to the sink and collected the scratch-art knives we needed. "I don't want to say," he responded once we sat down. He looked a bit embarrassed.

I sighed in frustration. "O–kay. You know, this whole Sydney thing could've been avoided if you had just picked another girlfriend by now. I mean seriously, it's been a month, hasn't it?"

"Five and a half weeks," Taylor grumbled.

"See? That creates too much talk. You need a girlfriend. You've never gone that long without one. If you already had one, Sydney wouldn't have asked you."

Taylor shook his head. "I'd rather not have a girlfriend right now. I really would just like to have a girl ask me to morp."

I caught the incredulous look that passed between Madison and Alyssa as they slipped into their chairs. *Yeah, they're probably really shocked right now. Kind of like I was about three minutes ago.*

"Okay," I tried again, "how about Emma? She would love to go with you."

"No."

I found one syllable answers could annoy me. "Why not?"

"I don't want to lead her on, you know?"

"Look, Taylor, what do you want from me? I'm trying to help you, okay?"

"I just don't want to go with Emma, all right?"

"So you already have a girl in mind, right? And you don't want to have just any girl ask you? You're only going to settle for this particular one?"

"Yes." He looked relieved.

"Great. Then who is it? I'm one hundred percent positive she'll say yes."

"I'm positive she won't want to go with me." He looked like a child whose Christmas gift had been stolen.

"Are we back to that again?" I exclaimed. "Sheez! Of course, she will want to go with you. Don't worry, I'll ask her. Believe me. She'll be all ecstatic and tell all of her friends. And—what? Why are you looking at me like that?"

Taylor's eyes really were the prettiest blue I had ever seen.

"Who are you taking to Morp?" he asked.

"Ah—I don't know yet. Someone who can dance," I hesitantly replied.

"Dance?"

"I don't mean like perfect or anything, but definitely not afraid to move."

"Why?"

"I love to dance. And if I'm spending money to take a guy to this thing, I want to know I'm going to have fun."

"Oh." Looking pensive, Taylor turned away. He glanced over at Madison and Alyssa and commented on their art work.

For a moment I just stared off into space as I debated his problem. "Hey, how about this!" I beamed. "It's perfect. I will ask you to morp. Then you can say you were asked."

"I—I can?" he stammered as his face lit up.

"Sure, with no strings attached. It's great! Then we can both go with who we really want."

His face fell. "I can't do that."

"Why?" *You are seriously beginning to bug me.*

"B–because it would be a lie," he answered. "I want to be asked for real. I don't want to lie."

"Well, sheez. If you don't tell me who this girl is and you won't let me just kind of pretend to ask you, then what in the world are you going to do?"

"I don't know. I need help."

More than you realize. "Taylor, I would love to help you, but I can't if all we're going to do is go round and round with this."

His gaze caught mine, and he took a breath that seemed almost nervous. "Chloe, I just want the girl to ask me for real."

I froze for a moment as I tried to decipher that gaze. And then it was like a light bulb exploded in my head. *Oh my gosh. He wants* me *to ask him. Me? How could I have been so dense? He can't be serious, can he? I can't. I'm not going to do it. No way. I can't even stand the guy. There is no way I can put up with him for a whole evening. I'd rather go out with Collin. He'll have to find someone else.* Silently, I turned away from Taylor and started to work on my art project.

{♥}

Jenni James

"You have to ask Taylor," Alyssa said. Her steps were hard put to keep up with mine as I rushed out of the art room after the bell rang. I was so intent on leaving as quickly as possible, I was surprised that Madison and Alyssa had caught up with me.

I was shocked. "I—I do?"

"Yes," Madison said. "Any fool could see he wanted *you* to ask him to morp."

"Are you sure? I mean, we all realize the significance of this dance. Maybe he hasn't thought it through properly." *There is no way he likes me.*

"Are you kidding me? Taylor has had five and a half weeks to think it through."

"Come on, you have to help him," Alyssa pleaded.

"He did help you with Mr. Young," Madison pointed out.

"Okay, yeah. But, that was forever ago." I shook my head.

"What about when he came to our party and was really funny and nice to everyone?" Madison tried again.

"And he paid for your dinner with Collin," Alyssa said.

"And he broke up with what's-her-name for you!"

"Anne," I mumbled.

"Yeah, well, he did," Madison said.

I had begun to cave. "But I can't stand Taylor. He's rude."

"When?" Alyssa challenged.

"Well, to Blake," I said.

Obviously, Madison wasn't impressed. "Where's Blake now?"

"Uh—" *Okay, so I can't fight that one.*

"Just ask him," Alyssa practically begged. "The guy is desperate. I don't know how many guys would've gone to the lengths he's has to try and convince you to like him."

"Put him out of his misery, please. It's just a dance." Now Madison sounded like she was begging as well. "You really

142

don't want to make him go to morp with Sydney, do you? No guy should ever have to do that."

Yeah, but this is Taylor we're talking about. He probably deserves it. "Are you really, really sure he's not trying to get back at me somehow?"

"No!" both girls almost hollered at me as we stopped in front of Mr. Young's class.

Nothing like being put on the spot. With a groan, I gave in. "Fine. Who sees him next?" I asked.

Madison said, "He's in Ms. Solomon's with me."

Alyssa ripped a sheet of notebook paper out of her binder, then handed me the sheet along with a glitter pen.

Sheez. Glitter?

"Write," she commanded.

After a second of hesitation I wrote:

T~

Will you go with me to morp?
It's for real this time

Chloe ❤

I was worried about putting the heart down. I didn't want Taylor to get any more ideas. But we had run out of time. And since I always drew a heart instead of writing "Hart," I figured it didn't matter.

"I'll make sure Taylor gets this." Alyssa smiled.

"Okay." I watched as she sealed my fate and put the note in her pocket. The bell rang. By the time I had walked into my English class Madison, and Alyssa were gone.

{♥}

I knew Taylor had gotten the note when he hollered from across the crowded hall after school, "Thank you, Copper Top!"

I could've died of embarrassment when everyone turned to look at me. Since it was Friday, it was a real good thing I wouldn't have to face anyone at school for three more days.

Later that night, Alyssa and Madison tormented me relentlessly. But all in all, they were really happy for me. By Sunday, I still hadn't told my parents. The only one of my family members who knew was Cassidy. I had hoped to talk to Taylor on Monday to go over details before I told anyone we were going together.

If I was completely honest with myself, I was surprised at how much I looked forward to morp—more than I thought I would. I was pretty darned excited about it, which was how I found myself as I practically ran to art class Monday morning: excited. I couldn't wait to see what Taylor thought of my ideas. But I didn't count on one small thing. I *wanted* to plan for morp, but I couldn't. Taylor wasn't there.

After roll call, Ms. Bailey made an announcement. "Taylor Anderson will no longer be in our art class."

What?

Maddi and Alyssa looked shocked too. By the gasps around the room, I realized we weren't the only ones who were surprised.

"He has transferred out of this class due to a schedule change," Ms. B. explained. "He will be attending art at another hour."

What? Why didn't he say anything? That's not like Taylor at all. You would think he would've had us all plan a farewell party in his honor. Didn't he know it was going to happen? Is this something last minute? And then an idea popped into my head. *Did he transfer because of me?*

That one sentence revolved in my head over and over again. *Did he transfer because of me? Did he transfer because of me? Did he . . . I need to leave.* The thought crossed my mind and furiously took hold. In moments I was up and facing Ms. B.

"Ms. Bailey? May I please go to the restroom?"

I barely heard her "sure" over the blood pounding in my ears.

Frantically, I grabbed the hall pass and fled to the privacy and sanctuary of the girl's bathroom. It was then that I realized Taylor had never said yes when I had asked him to morp. He had only said thank you. He had never really intended to go with me at all! This whole weekend, while I had stupidly dreamed and planned in my head all of the ridiculous things Taylor and I would do, they were just that—stupid, ridiculous dreams of a girl who should have known better. One small tear escaped and trailed down my cheek. I brushed it away. But in the very next breath I felt one on my other cheek. And then another and another. No matter how much I dashed and wiped and cursed my cheeks, the irrational tears still fell.

What am I crying for? It's not like I like Taylor anyway. He's popular, and in my wildest dreams I have never wanted to be popular. So stop. This is nonsense. Besides, maybe I'm being overdramatic. I don't know why Taylor left. See? I'm just jumping to conclusions. I'm sure he'll explain everything to me once he's given the chance. I hope.

A week later, I had lost all hope of Taylor explaining things to me, especially on Friday in art when I overheard Emma say excitedly to her friends, "Oh my gosh! You would not believe the outfits my stepdad just picked up for me! Taylor and I are going to look so amazing together at morp . . ."

He's going with Emma? She continued to babble, but I didn't need to hear the rest. I had heard enough. *Emma? The girl he didn't want to give false hopes to?*

The reality of what a fool I had made of myself began to sink in. I was the idiot I had vowed to never be. And it wasn't even Sydney he was going with. I maybe could've handled it if it was Sydney. But Emma?

I had visions of Taylor seeing my note and feeling about me just as he had felt when Sydney asked him. *Did I read everything wrong? Was I just flattering myself all along that he liked me? Did he leave our class because he was too chicken to tell me he didn't want to go with me?* It was obvious Taylor had avoided me. If he really wanted to find me he could've, just like any other day. It had been a whole week, and he had never even tried to contact me to tell me he had planned to go with someone else. That hurt more than anything. The least he could've done was pay me the courtesy of a rejection. I was so humiliated that when I came home from school Friday night, I went straight to my room and dropped on my bed.

Okay, so I know I'm not totally beautiful or anything. But man, there is nothing like going out on a limb only to find the guy you're out there for has a chainsaw and no safety net.

SEVENTEEN
♥
TAKE THAT!

After the initial shock of Taylor accepting Emma's invitation to morp, I finally snapped out of it and faced the facts. In other words, I got mad. I refused to allow Taylor Anderson to ruin my senior year—and subsequently my last morp—just because he was an idiot.

If I didn't show up at that dance with the hottest guy I could find, who could dance better than anyone there, I was in trouble. There was no way I was going to let Taylor think I was home wishing I could go to the dance with him. Just because he didn't accept my offer didn't mean I had to sit back and moan about it. At least I knew who Taylor was. I mean, how many times does a girl have to be jerked around by a guy, anyway? It was my own stupid fault for falling for his plea for help. Well, one thing was for sure. Taylor Anderson was going to wish he had gone to morp with me.

I would've totally asked Blake if he didn't already have a girlfriend. But he did. He would've been the perfect alternative, and he would've made Taylor mad, too. *Darn it.*

After about twenty-four hours of brainstorming, I remembered Jordan and Kate, the professional ballroom dancers from the theater last summer. I decided if I told Kate everything, she would talk Jordan into helping me. He wasn't the best-looking guy. I mean, Blake was way hotter. And Jordan's style of dancing was different, but I didn't care. He was older, so that was good. No one knew him—even better. And he was funny, which was perfect!

I was on the computer, emailing Kate, when Madison called.

"Oh, Maddi," I began, "I'm so excited you called. Guess who I'm going to ask to go to morp with me?"

"Uh, I don't know. Who?" She sounded a bit distracted.

"Jordan."

"Who?" Now she really sounded off.

"Oh, I forgot you don't know him. Never mind, I'll introduce you guys later. What's up?"

Madison cleared her throat. "I have some news of my own."

"Oh, cool. What is it?"

"I'm uh . . . well, I'm—I'm going to morp too."

"You are? That is so awesome. Who did you ask?"

"Well, uh, I asked—I mean, I invited . . . Collin Farnsworth."

I gasped. "Collin Farnsworth? Are you kidding?"

"No."

"But—but why?"

"Because I like him, okay?" Madison replied, sounding a little hurt.

My jaw hit the floor. "Wait a minute. You like Collin? Are you crazy? Why would you?"

"Just because you don't think he's worth your time, doesn't mean he's not a completely amazing guy. You're not the only one who—"

"Maddi, I am so sorry I upset you. If you truly like him, then please forgive me. I didn't mean to be so rude. I'm just shocked, that's all. I had no idea you liked him. If I did I wouldn't have said so many dreadful things all this time about him, you know?"

"Well, really, I was kind of hoping you would be happy for me. I'm not like you, okay? I mean, when was the last time I was even on a date?"

"I—I am happy for you," I declared. "When did you start liking him?"

"At our Halloween party. Once you get past his compliments and fancy phone, he really is a very nice guy. Plus he's totally cute. He's like my own Frog Prince." She giggled.

Madison giggling about a guy? She must really *like him.* "Frog Prince?" I smiled. "So are ya planning on kissing the guy anytime soon?"

"Hmm, maybe."

"Well, good luck with that. You'll have to tell me how it goes, okay?"

"Definitely." She laughed. "I'm so excited. I'm actually going to morp! I really didn't think I would go, and now I am."

Wow. Okay, so I am only the most selfish friend ever. I had no idea Madison would want to go. Morp was all I had talked about and complained of for weeks. And there was Madison as she supported and listened to me the whole time, wishing she could go too. Talk about a wake-up call. I decided right then to think more of others and less of myself. "Do you think Alyssa will come?" I asked.

"Oh, yeah," Madison said. "Last I heard she was going to ask someone from her orchestra class."

"If Jordan says yes, do you want to all go together?" If Collin and Madison were going to eventually hook up, I had better get used to the guy.

"Sure. That would be cool." She giggled again.

I had never heard Madison sound so happy before. I liked it.

We talked for a few more minutes, then hung up. I quickly finished my email to Kate. After a brief hesitation, I sent it off with a prayer. *Please, please, please, let Jordan agree to be my date. I know a girl shouldn't have pride and all, but I would really appreciate it if you let me keep some—just for morp, of course. I cannot let Taylor think I am home alone waiting and wishing for him.* And then for no reason at all, one very large tear rolled down my cheek. *Great.* All in all, I'd been way too emotional lately.

Jordan said yes!

I could've died, I was so happy—or relieved, whichever way you want to look at it. In the email to Kate, I'd told her everything about Taylor. She was so outraged that she was more than willing to help me. She told me I could borrow her boyfriend *and* her dance clothes. She even insisted she come over early Friday to do my hair and makeup. A whole makeover! Since we were about the same size and she already knew what her boyfriend slash dancing partner had in his closet, I had complete faith in her when she told me not to worry about a thing. I knew she was going to make me look fabulous.

And fabulous I looked. No, wait, make that more like sensational! Kate had brought over one of her Latin ballroom outfits. I was amazed at how nice it looked on me. Soon, Jordan arrived, wearing the black shirt that coordinated with mine. They both had these way cool Latiny flared sleeves. I loved the variegated skirt. It had Austrian crystals sewn throughout the lower part of it, and they twinkled and sparkled with every step

I took. I felt like a true fairy princess. I giggled and pranced and twirled all over the room just to see the crystals shine—until Kate told me I had to sit or she wouldn't have time to do my hair.

My hair! I could not believe the magic Kate had in her fingertips. Never in my life had I been able to transform my frizzy hair into such long, sumptuous curls. She said the secret was in the sculpting gel, but I own the stuff and have never produced that kind of results.

By the time Alyssa and Madison came over, I was so freakin' excited about morp I couldn't help myself. "Hi!" I gushed as I opened the door for them. "Oh my gosh! You two look awesome."

Madison had gone all country and had a cute button-up shirt, jeans, and a trendy straw cowboy hat. I wondered briefly how Collin would look in a cowboy outfit, but since he was cute anyway, I decided he wouldn't look half bad. Alyssa and the guy from orchestra had planned to go all '90s. She had come wearing a funky, multicolored rayon shirtdress with a wide butterfly-clasp belt. Totally vintage and way fun.

"Can you believe it's already time for morp? I'm so wound up I can't even see straight!" My smile was so large my cheeks were beginning to hurt, but I couldn't help myself.

Both girls took stock of my animated chatter with dazed expressions.

"What?" I asked as I paused to take a breath.

"Wow," Madison said.

"You look really pretty." Alyssa fidgeted with her purse in the entranceway of my house.

"Really?" I began to giggle again. "You've got to see this!" I twirled to show the sparkling crystals.

"Wow," Madison said again.

"That's really pretty," Alyssa added.

"All right." I put my hands on my hips. "What's up? Is something wrong?"

My two best friends shared a look before Maddi answered, "No. We just didn't expect you to be so chirpy to go to morp, that's all."

"Yeah," Alyssa said. "With Taylor and all, we'd expected you to be a little more down than you are."

"Are you kidding me?" I grinned. "I get to go to morp with a professional dancer. How much cooler is that than Taylor Anderson? Honestly, I haven't thought about Taylor all week." I decided to change the subject. "So when are the guys coming?"

Alyssa glanced at her watch. "In about five minutes."

"So where's this Jordan guy I keep hearing about?" Madison asked while craning her neck to see behind me.

"Oh, he's in the back room." I giggled. "Mom and Dad are putting him through a modified version of the Dating Ritual. You really don't want to go back there yet. Come in my room and meet Kate."

{♥}

Morp was magical. I had never been to a school dance where I felt this amazing. My hair, my makeup, my clothes, my date—everything was perfection. Even junior prom didn't feel this good. Tonight I was alive, happy, and so excited. I knew it would be a night to remember. I could feel it.

Thanks to one of my strappy sandals that came undone just as we were getting out of the car, Jordan and I entered the gym after the rest of the group. Everyone turned and stared at us, and I could tell many of the girls wondered who he was. His aura by far made up for whatever he lacked in the looks category. I don't know how it works, but in a world where image is everything, Jordan created his own. He *believed* he was hot, so everyone else thought so as well. I felt so proud and beautiful to be on his arm as I walked into our decorated gymnasium.

About fifteen minutes into the dance, I realized that a worse deejay did not exist on the planet. I guess the money spent for a prom fundraiser couldn't be wasted on a good deejay. Most of the music was ten years old or more. Don't get me wrong—the Backstreet Boys and N'Sync are legends in their own right, but honestly, at a high school dance? All night? *Yuck.*

The dance floor was packed, so packed I couldn't see everyone. Jordan and I had totally lost our group. The worst part was no one was really dancing because the music was so terrible.

"What do you want to do?" Jordan finally asked. Obviously, the dance was completely inferior to anything he was used to.

I felt bad for him. "I don't know. Should we go?" I knew it had to be awkward for him to be at a high school dance anyway, and to be at one where people just stood around and gossiped had to be torture.

"You know what?" Jordan grinned. "I have a better idea. Look behind us."

Except for a few people taking pictures by the photo scene, there was basically no one in the back corner of the gym. "What?" I said. "I don't get it."

He pointed to the empty part of the gym. "Look, that's a huge dance floor just waiting to be danced on. No one is using it. So what do ya say? You want me to teach you some more ballroom moves?"

"Are you kidding me? Here? Now?" The idea had begun to make me smile, too.

"Sure why not?" He laughed. "It's not like anyone is looking back there anyway."

He had a point. "Can we?" I asked. "Even with this music on?"

"Sure. You can find rhythm in all types of music. You just have to listen for the beat." He grabbed my hand and began to pull me toward the back. "Come on, I'll show you."

So that is how I came to be ballroom dancing at the back of the gym during our high school's morp. I didn't care if anyone saw us. It was so much fun. Jordan taught me advanced moves for the waltz, tango, cha-cha, rumba, and my personal favorite, the jive. I laughed so hard as we dipped and swayed along the back of the room that I didn't even notice the attention we had attracted.

That was until about two-thirds of the way through the night, when Jordan asked, "So which guy is Taylor?"

"What?" I was confused.

"Taylor Anderson. I didn't grow up here, remember? Which one is he?" Then Jordan spun us around to give me a view of the crowd that was watching us, which included almost everyone there! Shocked, I stumbled a bit, but in an expert move, he bent with me and smoothed over it to make the trip look like part of the dance.

It didn't take long for me to pick out Taylor from the large group. He must've been standing there for a while, because he was in a pretty relaxed pose as he stared right at me. Thankfully, Jordan broke my connection with Taylor's eyes as he spun me out into an extended spin—an extended spin that brought me approximately three feet from a very sulky Emmalee Bradford. *Oops!* Evidently she wasn't too happy to spend her morp in the back of the gym as she listened to lousy music and watched me dance. I didn't blame her.

And then I was gone, whisked into a series of rotations that brought me next to Jordan again. It was the most exhilarating experience, and he made me feel so, well, light.

"Taylor is the guy standing there in the red shirt," I replied a little breathlessly.

"Yep. I figured it was him. That guy has not taken his eyes off you since we started dancing."

"Really?" My steps faltered again.

Jordan effortlessly matched my pace and chuckled. "You sure he doesn't like you? Kate said a bunch of stuff, but I'm not buying it. That, my friend, looks like a man in love."

I gulped. "In love?" I couldn't help myself; I turned my head to see Taylor.

"Whoa. Watch your step. There." He spun me in the opposite direction of Taylor.

I didn't even know I had messed up that time. "Sorry. Thanks."

"So is that pretty li'l blond, the girl, then?" He laughed. "The one folding her arms and looking madder than a bull in Spain?"

"Yes. I feel bad." I glanced back at Taylor again.

"Don't look at him," Jordan ordered. "Look right at me."

"Why?"

"Chloe. Look into my eyes. There. Keep focused."

They were brown. I didn't know Jordan had brown eyes. And now they were laughing at me. "What?" I grinned.

"Good. Keep looking at me and smiling. Very good."

My smile grew. "Are you gonna answer me or what?"

"Do you want to make him jealous or what?" Jordan did a series of quick whirls that brought me up close to his side. I looked right into his eyes.

"Good girl. Very good. If you want to know what Taylor is doing, just ask me. I get to look at him, but you don't.

Understand? And believe me, I'm having more fun smiling at Taylor than I thought I would. He really doesn't like me. Now just make sure your focus is on me." We did three backward steps and then another series of twirls that brought my hip next to his other side. I stayed completely focused on Jordan.

I couldn't stand it. "Okay. What's he doing?" I intently studied the back of Jordan's neck as he glanced over at Taylor.

After another group of breathtakingly fast-paced twirls, I was in front of Jordan again. One of his hands held my waist as he lowered me down for a dip.

Dip? We didn't practice a dip!

Jordan's leg slid as he lunged forward and allowed me to fall back more. He was in complete control. And so after my brief panic, I relaxed and trusted him. "He wishes he was in your arms already," I heard Jordan whisper as my head fell back to enjoy the world upside down. With another twirl, Jordan's hands encircled my waist as he spun me in an effortless lift back to standing position. "I have never seen such a hungry look on anyone's face before. No—no, don't look. Stare right at me." The music ended. "Now laugh," he directed.

"I am laughing." I giggled.

"Good girl." He chuckled and then looked at Taylor. I thought I saw him wink. Jordan looked back at me. "That boy is putty in your hands."

EIGHTEEN

♥

BETRAYAL AND DENIAL

Saturday morning at 10:00 found me luxuriously lying in my bed as I ignored everything I had to do. My mind raced with thoughts of the dance the night before. The whole way home, Alyssa and Madison had praised Jordan nonstop for his dancing abilities and how we were the only thing that made the dance worth attending. I laughed to myself at the memory of Jordan's imitation of Taylor, performed for us on the way home. *Good. Taylor deserves to see what it's like to want something.* I smiled again and stretched my wiggling toes, thinking of Madison and her date, Collin.

Collin had handled being around me pretty well. I mean, there was a brief awkwardness at the beginning of the evening when we all met at my house, but nothing like what I thought it would be. I guess my dad was right. For the most part, Collin managed to avoid talking to me at all by playing with his phone.

Alyssa seemed to enjoy herself. I could tell she wasn't too impressed with her friend from the orchestra class, but he was nice. I think they were one of the only other couples who actually danced to a few songs.

I was so busy with Jordan in the back of the gym that I really didn't see much of anyone else at the dance. We did all get together and have our picture taken at the very end, which was cool. I was glad I would have something to remind myself of morp.

"Chloe?" My mom knocked on my door. "You've got a phone call."

"Come in," I called as I sat up.

"Here." Mom handed me the phone. "Don't talk too long, okay? We've got chores today."

"All right." I nodded my head. I waited until my mom had left the room before I said, "Hello?"

"Hi, beautiful." It was Blake.

Unprepared for his deep voice, I couldn't contain the shudders that sizzled down my back. I was a little stunned that he still had the same effect on me.

"Hi. Long time no talk," I improvised.

"Miss me bad?" he teased.

What does he want? "Nope, not as bad as you wish I had. So what's up?"

"Knowing how much you despise Taylor, I thought you'd be interested to learn something new about your friend Alyssa, something I learned last night."

Alyssa? "Is it good or bad?"

"Bad."

My chest tightened up. "Bad? What do you mean?"

"I mean it's not good. It's bad."

"Blake!" I almost shouted. "Get on with it."

"I know why Zack broke up with Alyssa."

I gasped. "You do? Why? What happened?"

"Taylor."

"Excuse me?"

"Taylor. Taylor broke them up."

My mind raced with a hundred questions, but I only managed to get two out. "What do you mean? H–how do you know?"

"He told me last night when he came to the hotel after some dance."

"He told *you?*" I couldn't believe it.

"Yeah. Well, okay, it was more like he told Zack. But I could hear every word."

"How? What did he say? How did it happen?"

"Well, he came in fuming last night. I guess the dance didn't go like he thought it would. I don't know. But after his normal rude greeting to me he stomped into his dad's office and slammed the door."

I frowned into the receiver.

"Then he came right back out again," Blake continued, "demanding to know where his dad was. I told him he'd left hours ago and pointed out it was after 11:00 p.m. Taylor seemed really surprised at the time. He even started to laugh."

He started to laugh?

"After a few seconds, he calmed down a bit. He told me he was looking for his cell phone. He asked if his dad had left it with me or if he'd taken the phone home with him. I told him I hadn't seen it. Then he stomped back into his dad's office, and this time he left the door open as he dialed Zack's number from the office phone, which is how I overheard what he said to Zack. Taylor was totally going on and on about how good it was that Zack had broken up with Alyssa, and how it was a good thing Zack took his advice and listened to him about breaking up with her."

"But why?" I moaned. "Why would he do that? Did he say?"

"All I could make out from the conversation was that Taylor didn't like Alyssa. And he definitely didn't think his friend Zack should, either. After that Taylor must've realized the door was wide open because the next thing I heard was it slam shut. About twenty minutes later, Taylor stormed out of the hotel and drove away."

Oh my gosh.

My heart nearly stopped for Alyssa—my friend who almost always defended Taylor. My friend who would never say a bad word about anyone. To be so insulted by him, and to Zack, of all people. It was horrible. No, it was worse than horrible. It was malicious.

"Chloe?" Blake's voice on the other end of the phone startled me. "Are you all right?"

"Yes. I'm fine," I replied. "I've just got a headache all of a sudden. I'm going to go, okay? Thanks for letting me know. Bye." I hung up the phone before I had even heard Blake's answering farewell.

I began to pace in my room, trying to figure out why Taylor didn't like Alyssa. Weren't we all sort of friends? He'd always been nice to her. How could someone be so nice to someone's face and then so utterly cold behind her back? And to ruin a relationship—that was beyond anything I could bear. *The nerve. Taylor Anderson is such a chicken butt!*

All at once, the room began to close in on me, and I wanted out. In a fury, I changed from my pajamas into jeans and a T-shirt. I grabbed my slip-on Vans and jacket from the closet and headed out of my bedroom.

Within seconds, I slammed the front door behind me, then ran across the street to our neighborhood park. It was pretty much empty, thank goodness, apart from some boys playing baseball in the adjoining field. So far it was still too early in the morning for little kids to venture outside in late January.

I walked over to my favorite swing and plunked down on it. Then I took off my shoes and watched my feet as they squished in the cold sand. It was really cold sand, but I didn't care. The sand wasn't any colder than my heart felt.

Alyssa. Poor Alyssa. Why her? How could Taylor not like her? She is the sweetest, nicest, most wonderful girl in the world. It isn't fair. She deserves so much better than I do.

"Chloe?"

Jolted from my musings, I looked up into the beguiling blue eyes of Taylor Anderson. I wondered if I was imagining things. "You?" was all I could get out.

"Sorry." I watched Taylor's lips move, but it took a moment to comprehend what he was saying. ". . . parked at your house . . . came over when I saw you—"

"Oh." My voice cracked, and all I could think was, *What is he doing here?*

"Are you okay? You don't look so hot." Taylor's concern for me frustrated me more.

I was okay until you *showed up.* "I—I'm fine." To prove it, I went to stand up, but I had forgotten my shoes were off and I tripped over them in the process. Had it not been for Taylor catching me, I would have landed in an unflattering heap at his feet. Again.

He chuckled in my ear as he wound his arms around me. The side of my face was pressed into his coat. His cologne began to tickle my senses. "Are you sure you're okay?" His breath stirred the fine hairs above my ear and warmed my cold cheek below it.

He gave such an impression of strength and security. Had I not known what a villain he was, I would've been tempted to stay in his arms forever. "Excuse me," I mumbled as I detached myself from him. Almost as an afterthought I added, "Thank you," once we were apart.

Taylor stepped back so I could pick up my shoes. In silence, he watched as I sat back on the swing and brushed my feet off before slipping the Vans on again. Then I dusted my hands on my jeans and stood up.

What do you want? I thought, unable to get my mouth to say the words. He just stood there and watched me. *Fine. Don't talk then.* In my irritation, I moved away and stood by the large row of steps that led to the slide. I looked out at the boys playing baseball. There were so many things I wanted to tell Taylor, but not now. I needed a few more days before I went all postal on him. Right then I really didn't want to talk to anyone, least of all him. *Maybe he'll just go away if I ignore him.*

The silence loomed for several minutes, and soon I wondered if he had gone. I refused to turn around and see. In fact, my back was still to him when he finally spoke.

"Chloe, I had to come see you."

I stiffened my back and raised my head in defiance.

"I'm going crazy here," he said in a frustrated tone. "I can't sleep, I can't concentrate in school—everything's a mess. Listen, I don't know who that guy was you were dancing with, but please, you've gotta hear me out." I heard a faint mutter and then a ragged sigh before Taylor half whispered, "I—I love you." It was like a dam had burst. In the next breath he was louder, much louder. "I do. I have loved you from the first time I saw you stomp away from those bleachers three and a half years ago. And trust me, I've tried to get over it, always moving on to new girlfriends, pretending like you meant nothing—like I wasn't in love with you—but I can't do this anymore. You're the only girl I want. Chloe, I need you to go out with me."

In shock, I stood rooted to the ground, facing the same playing field Taylor faced. I knew I had to say something. I lowered my head and contemplated my hands for a moment before I bravely squared my shoulders. Slowly, I turned toward him. He still stood by the swing. His raw uncertainty disarmed me a little as his anguished eyes searched mine for an answer. I knew at that moment that Taylor thought he loved me. But he didn't, not really. *He has never loved me,* I decided. *He just loves the* idea *of me—of having the one girl who doesn't worship the ground he walks on.* But I couldn't love him. I *wouldn't* love him. With a deep breath, I braced myself.

"Taylor, thank you." *There, that sounded good.* "But no."

For several long moments, he stared at me, obviously confounded. At first, I wasn't sure he had heard me. Finally, he spat out, "That's all you're going to say? That's it?" He moved a step closer to the swing and yanked its chain toward him. "You'd think that when a guy bares his soul to a girl at least she would give him a proper reply. Not some stiff, harsh, monotone rejection." His anger was evident as he punctuated each adjective with a jerk of the swing.

Disgusted, I put my hands on my hips. "Proper reply? You mean yes, right?"

"I don't care what answer you give. Just give me a reason. If you actually have one, that is."

"Are you kidding me?" I said furiously. "I was only trying to be nice. You want to know what I really think about you? Fine, let me spell out all my reasons. First off, Taylor Anderson, what makes you think I would ever consider becoming the girlfriend of the guy who has crushed one of my best friends? Zack and Alyssa. Can you say it wasn't you who broke them up? And that you told—no make that *commanded*—Zack to leave Alyssa?"

Taylor looked confused, then angry. "You better believe I broke them up. I take care of my friends more than I am able to take care of myself. At least I was able to stop him from falling for someone who couldn't care less about him."

Jerk! Imbecile! Moron! "But that's not all!" I blurted. "You know it isn't. What about Blake Winter—Wilder—your own cousin?"

"Blake? How much has he told you?"

"You tried to get him fired. You're a jealous, attention-seeking jerk who would try to undermine his own cousin, just so you could have what you wanted, just to make sure no one shared your spotlight."

"Wow! So that's what you think of me?" Taylor shook his head. "You don't really know what's going on, and you don't even care. You know why? Because you're a fraud, Chloe Hart. Yep. You go ahead and stand there and think how much better you are than the popular crowd, but you know what? You're just as bad as they are. We both know that you'd rather die than admit the only thing stopping you from going out with me is that I'm popular. The next time you're out somewhere flinging accusations at people, check your double standard first."

"My double standard?" *Look in the mirror, buddy!* I stormed up to the swing. It was the only thing separating us as I looked up into his face. "Taylor, you are the most conceited, rudest, most arrogant *boy* I have ever had the misfortune of meeting. I would never in a million years go out with you. Even if you had never hurt Blake or Alyssa, you'd still be a smug, manipulating jock with no regard for anybody else's feelings. Never mind morp and getting me to ask you just—just so you could humiliate me. When I first moved here I saw what a complete jerk you were, thinking you owned everything and everyone. Well, you don't own me, and you never will. I deserve someone much better than you!"

The air positively crackled as the hollow reminder of my words echoed around us. Taylor slowly scanned my face, his eyes a dull gray. I cannot begin to imagine what emotions he saw there.

He took a step back and then another from the swing that separated us. Then he paused before nodding briefly. "Thank you, Chloe. It's nice to know what someone really thinks of you. Sorry for wasting your time."

And then Taylor Darcy Anderson walked away.

NINETEEN
♥
A DIFFERENT SIDE

I collapsed into the swing after Taylor was gone, completely bereft of emotion and energy. And then I did what any sensible girl would do in my situation—I leaned my head against the hand holding the swing chain and cried.

It was some time later that I realized how cold I was. Grasping the chains, I lifted myself off the swing. My limbs felt stiff so I wrapped my jacket closer, then stomped to get the blood moving in my legs and feet. With one deliberate step at a time, I slowly made my way back across the sand and onto the concrete sidewalk, then across the street to my house. Down the street to my right I could see Alyssa's and Madison's homes. The sun seemed to happily bounce off them, and they represented a beacon of comfort I couldn't indulge in at present. I walked the rest of the twenty or so yards to my front door with a determination to get on with my day.

The next day, Sunday, my mother saw my peaked and weary face and told me to go back to bed. The rest of the family went to church without me. Before they left, my dad came into my room to see how I was doing. He brought his laptop with him and told me not to tell Mom.

"It's just so you won't get cabin fever while we're gone," he teased, and then after a moment, he added, "Yesterday, I saw the Anderson boy's sports car in front of our house for a while. It wouldn't have anything to do with your hiatus to the park yesterday morning, would it?"

"Well, yeah, it did," I answered. *In a roundabout way.*

"Is that boy sweet on you?"

I looked down and shook my head. "Not anymore." My finger rubbed along the soft nose of the bear I was holding.

"Kicked him to the curb, did ya?" He chuckled.

I tried to smile. "Yeah."

"Chloe?"

"Yeah?" I looked up at my dad.

"Listen here. I'm not going to make some big speech about popular boys and the nuisance they are, because thankfully you've got a better head on your shoulders than that. I know you're smart enough to make your own decisions, without your dad buggin' you about them. But there is one thing."

"Okay?"

Dad took a deep breath. "Don't go judging people on what you hear alone. I hope you always give every boy who comes here a fair chance to prove himself to you." He raised his hands. "Now, I'm not saying anything about that Anderson fellow. I don't know what happened. And by the look of you the past twenty-four hours, I don't think I want to." He walked over to my dresser and leaned against it. "But in saying that, I have to point out that Taylor's a good boy. I've seen him around this town helping many folks. And as far as I can see he does it in his free time, too. I've personally witnessed him doing everything from shingling widows' roofs to mowing the lawn at the homeless shelter. He even organized and ran the city's trash pickup last summer while you were practicing for your play.

"Every time I've seen that boy, there's a smile on his face, until yesterday when he got into his car and drove off. Again, I'm not trying to interfere here. I'm sure you've got reason enough to do what you did. Actually, I know you do. You're a good girl. I'm just saying that if ever you do change your mind, no one's gonna judge you for it."

Dumbfounded, I stared at my dad as he rose from the dresser. "Well, I'm off to church. Don't go all crazy on me now, you hear?" He laughed at his attempt at a joke.

"Thanks, Dad." I smiled back at him, a little perplexed.

I watched as he winked at me and then shut the door halfway behind him. Then I looked down at the laptop on the end of my bed and smiled ruefully. *My daddy loves me.*

I really wasn't feeling well, and I wasn't quite sure I even wanted to touch the computer. But I was wide awake. All I could think about was that conversation with Taylor. There were so many more things I wished I'd said—and so many I wished I hadn't. My dad kind of siding with Taylor didn't make sense to me, either. I mean my dad was an amazing judge of character, and I was surprised he saw Taylor in the same light as the rest of the town.

After about thirty minutes, I couldn't take the solitude of the house anymore. I flipped open the laptop and let it boot up. I decided to check my email and maybe send a few messages to the people I'd neglected lately.

I was writing a thank-you email to Jordan and Kate when I received a message in my inbox. It was from Taylor. *Oh my gosh! How did he get my email address?*

Then I remembered the school website contained a list of students' email addresses—everyone who didn't mind being part of a public listing, that is. I had put mine on there a couple of years ago. Now that I thought about it, I could've probably gotten Taylor's email address the same way. Not that I needed to—his email address was staring right at me: ta2h0t2hndl@gmail.com.

I was loath to read his email, yet so curious I couldn't help myself. My heart sped up as I clicked on it. The subject simply read, "Yesterday."

Once the email loaded, I scanned it and was shocked at how long it was. I settled back against my pillows and the headboard of my bed, then brought the PC closer to rest on my crossed legs. I read through the letter once and then, agitated, read the whole thing again.

From: Taylor Anderson <ta2h0t2hndl@gmail.com>
Subject: Yesterday

Chloe,

Hi. Before you read more, I just wanted to say, don't be worried that this email is in any way me begging to be with you again. I wouldn't want to disgust you more. It's obvious that you're not into me.

I've thought back on our argument yesterday and wanted to email you about the reasons why you're so mad at me. I think an explanation is needed. I realize now that you never really knew me, or took the time to get to know me. That leads perfectly into your accusations about Blake. My cousin is not the perfect guy you seem to think he is. In fact he's more a villain than a hero. During high school, Blake was always caught doing something. Drugs, drinking, stealing—you name it, he did it. Then a year ago, Blake went on trial in Colorado for drugging a fifteen-year-old girl and then taking advantage of her. He was eighteen at the time, and she was a minor. The trial went on for a while but nothing was ever proven. Blake got off scot-free, and my family tried their best to keep it under wraps and just forget the whole thing. But no one in Boulder would give him a chance. So his mom (my dad's sister) called and begged my dad to give Blake a job and a place to live. ←Hence the job at the hotel, which includes room and board.

Right before your Halloween party, I learned Blake had changed his last name to Winter and that my father had helped finance it so my cousin could make a new start for himself. To say I was livid was an understatement. I went completely ballistic and got in a huge fight over it with my dad. I was concerned that with the changed name, no one would recognize Blake and keep their daughters away from him, just in case he tried something here. Plus there was the added fact that you were seeing him. (I was so worried about you then—you have no idea.) You will probably be mad to learn that I warned Blake off you. I won't tell you all I said, but it got the message across.

Moving on, I did break up Zack and Alyssa. But I did it to protect my friend. Since sometime last summer, all I have heard about from him in every conversation was the beautiful Alyssa Ming, the cello player. Zack had become so obsessed with her I thought he would lose his mind. He's kind of uncomfortable around girls —more than me, at least ;). But besides that he's had a rough time of it since his mom's death. For almost ten years I've watched Zack slowly come out of his shell again. And it wasn't until Alyssa that I had seen him so happy.

Except there was a problem. Alyssa never talked about Zack like he did her, <u>ever.</u> Not once during art did she even mention him. Yet every day after school Zack asked if she had talked about him. So I had begun to think that maybe she didn't like him the way he liked her, but it wasn't until the Halloween party that I knew I was right. Zack stared at her and followed her wherever she went, but Alyssa barely even acknowledged him. Sure she stood next to him and they talked a little bit, but it wasn't anything that made me think she liked him. I felt after that night that Zack was seriously making a fool of himself over her. I was worried, because she reminded him so much of his mother, that he may have a relapse again if Alyssa broke his heart. Shortly after that, I convinced him to break up with her and to move on and try to find someone else.

When morp came along, I think he was still foolishly hoping she'd ask him, and of course, she didn't. It was right after morp that I was finally able to tell him that she had at least moved on and that she went with another guy, who she seemed to have a great time with. Anyway, that's what happened, and I did what I did because I thought it was the best thing for him.

Speaking of morp, I would like to explain my actions, which you threw at me yesterday. While you may or may not have cared whether I went with you to morp, I did.

(Let me reiterate that I <u>did</u>.) After you left art class and made it obvious by your silence that you were not going to ask me to morp, Emma asked me to go with her. Because I was desperate and she was a much better alternative to Sydney, I agreed right then and thanked her.

When Alyssa handed me your note the next hour, I panicked. I didn't know what to do. I knew you were expecting a positive answer, but I had just promised Emma I would go with her. At the time, the only person in the world I wanted to ask me was you, and you did. I had planned on telling you everything right after school, but I couldn't bring myself to. It was what I wanted more than anything. Besides, who knew, maybe something would happen and Emma would change her mind.

I began to panic that weekend when I realized I would have to face you and tell you I couldn't go with you. I couldn't bear to have you ask me questions about morp. So I transferred out. After a couple of weeks, I knew it was too late to tell you we weren't going together. I mean, it would've been useless and rude after so much time. (At least that is what I convinced myself.) It was stupid, I know. It was probably one of the dumbest things I have ever done. I am sorry for acting so immaturely or selfishly (as you put it) in that instance. For that I will apologize. But the rest, there is no apology. I did what I thought was best.

Take care,
Taylor

I couldn't believe he didn't think Alyssa liked Zack. She was crazy for him! I refused to even think about the rest of the letter at the moment, but in regards to Alyssa, I decided to set the record straight. *How dare he decide if someone likes someone or not! Ooh!* I clicked the reply button and started to type. After I deleted three different greetings to Taylor, I finally decided not to include one.

From: Chloe Hart <chlo3hart@yahoo.com>
Subject: Yesterday

For your information, Alyssa is shy. And just because she doesn't want to talk about Zack in front of his best friend doesn't mean she doesn't talk about him in front of her best friends. She talks about him all the time! She still doesn't understand what she did wrong. You know nothing about girls, Taylor. It baffles me that a guy who has been in as many relationships as you have, still does not understand the simple fundamental basics of women. How dare you say that one of my best friends was never in love with Zack! How dare you say that she did not care for him! You weren't even there the day he broke up with her. I was. I saw the tears and grief from that girl. Why do guys think they have the answer to everything?

Chloe

P.S. Alyssa is not in a relationship, and she has most decidedly not *moved on. Not that that little fact will fix anything, but I wanted to set the record straight.*

TWENTY
♥
VALENTINE SURPRISES

I never got a reply from Taylor, and after a couple of weeks, I gave up waiting for one. Obviously, the guy had said what he wanted to say. To say I was shocked over Blake's past would be a serious understatement. After I read Taylor's email over and over again, I was able to remember and piece together conversations with Blake that made more sense now.

I hated to admit it, but in my gut I knew Taylor was right. Blake was a villain—a nasty, despicable, horrid criminal. I was grateful for Taylor's interference and warning Blake away from me. I couldn't believe I'd blatantly disregarded and dismissed Taylor as a womanizer and found myself nearly in the snares of one. *It was Blake's stupid dimples. Guys should never have dimples.* Okay, so it was more than that, and I knew it. Blake's charming personality and flattering attention had drawn me in like a moth to a flame.

The irony of the situation was not lost to me. All along I had considered Taylor to be playing a game, while I was positive that Blake was serious about me, when in actual fact it was Blake playing the game, and Taylor was the one who was serious. *Taylor? Taylor Anderson really and truly loved me. For three years he had loved me.* That statement still continued to baffle me, no matter how many times I repeated the words in my head.

I couldn't imagine how much he hated me now. I had said some pretty unforgiving things to him. I wouldn't blame him at all if he never wanted to speak to me again. Not that I wanted to talk to him. I was convinced Taylor was still as conceited as ever—maybe not such a jerk, but definitely conceited. Of course, my opinion of him changed just a bit more on Valentine's Day.

On Monday, Madison, Alyssa, and I were all in art class together when the florist arrived and delivered a package to Alyssa. It was the largest collection of roses I had ever seen. There had to have been at least six dozen red and white roses. The note attached just said one word, "Will."

At first, we all thought a guy named Will had sent them, at least until the next delivery came about five minutes after the first. In walked a deliveryman carrying six extra-large heart-shaped boxes full of chocolates. The whole class freaked. The excitement and buzz that came from everyone as the man set them in front of Alyssa could've launched a rocket, it was so energetic. There was a card attached to the top box that read, "You."

It didn't take Madison, Alyssa, and I long to put the two words together, which was good, since the next deliveryman brought a dozen metallic, heart-shaped helium balloons. The front balloon was big and shaped like a bee. It was really cute. It was Madison who noticed the small note attached to the bee balloon that read, "Be."

I had never seen a spread like the one on our table. Art was completely forgotten. Everyone in the class was anxious for the next delivery. Even Ms. Bailey was eager. She actually walked out and stared down the hall so she could see what would come next. We knew when the next delivery had made it into the building because Ms. B. got all flustered and ran back to her desk.

This time it was a gigantic white teddy bear that dwarfed the whole deliveryman. When he walked in with it, all we could make out were his two jean-covered legs beneath it. The bear had a large card wrapped around its neck with a ribbon. The front of the card read, "Mine?"

The guy carrying the bear walked cautiously into the room and then stopped. I looked down at his shoes and thought they looked familiar.

When I heard Alyssa gasp, I looked up to see Zack's head as he peeked around the bear. Just then the whole room gasped, and I could hear exclamations of "Zack Bradford?" and "No way!" or "It can't be!"

Alyssa's chair scraped against the floor as she ran to throw her arms around Zack's side. Immediately, he dropped the bear at his feet and scooped her up in a hug. He even spun her around and everything. The smile on her face could've outshone the sun. Then Zack did the most unbelievable thing ever. He set Alyssa's feet on the ground and kissed her, right in front of the whole class and Ms. Bailey. It was awesome. We all hooted and hollered and caused such a disturbance that some students from the other classes came in to see what the commotion was about.

Thank you, Taylor Anderson. I was so happy for Alyssa, I almost cried. I looked at Ms. B., who was discreetly wiping at her cheeks. It would seem our teacher had a romantic side we never knew about.

Alyssa wasn't the only one to be surprised on Valentine's Day. Collin had also planned something special for Madison.

Since Zack intended to drive Alyssa home—he let us know he was never letting her out of his sight again—Madison and I took off right after school. She was really excited and wanted to get changed before Collin got to her house. Apparently the time of the surprise wasn't a surprise, because she knew he would be there at precisely 3:35.

Once I got home it hit me that I had nothing really particular to do that day except teach my dance class. I was so happy for my friends and their Valentine dates that it left hardly anything for me to pity myself over. Okay, I am human, and I did wonder what it would've been like for me, had Taylor been my boyfriend. Would he have surprised me with loads of gifts like Zack, in front of the whole room? Or would he have taken me somewhere nice and romantic that didn't cost a dime? Personally, I am for the nice romantic stuff, but a card or box of chocolates wouldn't have gone amiss. *What am I thinking? There's no use regretting something I can't change. Besides, he'll never notice me again anyway. Why would he when he has a whole slew of girls waiting to be his?*

Obviously, my little pep talk would've worked a whole lot better if I didn't have a new reminder of Taylor to contend with twice a week. My own personal Valentine surprises consisted of two very separate things:

Surprise one: Ms. Chavez had told me as soon as I walked into the studio that she had received a phone call that morning from her friend, who said the audition committee had recently reviewed my audition tape. I had been accepted into the ballet scholarship program in Arizona State University next fall!

Surprise two: I also had a charming new four-year-old ballet student by the name of Georgia Anderson. Luckily for me, Mrs. Anderson enrolled her daughter in my dance class the one day

I found the hardest to dismiss Taylor from my thoughts. *Really, this whole "fates set against me" thing is getting a little hard to live with.*

The little blond girl was adorable. She only reminded me of Taylor when she smiled, laughed, or looked at me with her sky blue eyes. And it took about four weeks for my heart to stop beating erratically in simultaneous dread and hope that Taylor might decide to drop her off or pick her up from class. Since he never showed up and his mother always did, I eventually began to chastise myself for ever thinking he might've shown an interest in his sister's ballet school, or more importantly, her teacher. I never stopped looking out in the hallway for him, but I did stop expecting him to be there.

As the days passed I got attached to Georgia, who had fast become one of my favorite students. Not only did she amaze me with how quickly she picked up ballet, but I also loved how kind she was to the other girls. The longer I taught her, the more I saw in her a reflection of her family.

I had to admit I had probably misjudged the Andersons. Not only did it seem that they taught good principles to their daughter, but she never once looked down on the other children and she was constantly encouraging them with compliments. Many days I would watch little Georgia share with or bring presents to her new friends. One week, she brought pretty princess ballerina stickers for all of the girls. Another week it was sparkly ribbons for their hair. And for the week of St. Patrick's Day, it was a plateful of four-leaf-clover-shaped cookies that she and Taylor had made.

"Wow, Georgia." I gasped as I held the plate. "Did you and Taylor really make all of these?"

"Yep." Her blond curls bounced up and down. "Taylor even let me stir 'em an' frost 'em!"

Curious about this different side of Taylor, I asked, "Does he always make cookies with you?"

"Yep, when he's home he does."

"When he's home?"

"Yep. It's been wheelly fun, cuz he's home more now cuz he broke-ed up wif his gill-friend." She bounced from one foot to the other.

"Did he have a new one?" I asked.

"Not since Kylie. She didn't not like me anyways. She never let me frost da cookies if Taylor wasn't not lookin'."

"Really? That's not nice." I frowned. *Maybe Kylie is more mean than I thought.*

"Yeah, Taylor found out 'bout it an' he got mad." Georgia did a little spin in place and watched her skirt twirl around her.

"Because she wouldn't let you frost cookies?"

"No, cuz she didn't not like me."

"Oh." *Yeah, I can see that not going over very well with Taylor.*

Georgia held one of my hands. "I like you, though."

I looked down at her smiling face. "You do?"

"Yep. I told Taylor you should be his gill-friend, cuz I like-ed you so much."

I choked out, "Y—you did?"

"Yep."

"Does he know who I am?"

"Oh, yeah. He says you're da best dancer in da whole world!"

"He did?"

"Yep. That's why I told him you should be his gill-friend, cuz you can dance so good."

"What did Taylor say?" *Oh my gosh. What did he say?*

"About what?" Georgia dropped my hand.

"Um, about you wanting me to be his girlfriend."

"Oh, he said you didn't not like him."

"He did?"

"Yep. Is that true? You don't not like my brov-ur?" Her Taylor-blue eyes pled with mine.

"I, uh, no, it's not true."

"So you like him!" Georgia began to jump up and down.

"Um, of course. Your brother's very nice." I gently placed my hand on her head, trying to calm her.

"Yeah. He does nice stuff for lots of people." She began to sway back and forth under my hand as she watched her skirt swish.

"So, um, do you know why your brother doesn't have a girlfriend?"

Swish, swish. "Nope. He says he can't not have one wight now."

"Why?"

She shrugged. "I dunno. That's just what he says."

"Is that why your mom comes and picks you up and not Taylor?"

"I dunno." Georgia began to jump again. "Can I pass the cookies to ev-we-one? Please, please, please?"

So much for getting more info. I laughed. "Sure."

TWENTY-ONE
♥
MY OWN PEMBERLEY

It was the end of March when I noticed Georgia had left her dance bag at the studio. After a brief hesitation, I decided to take it over to the Anderson home. I knew Georgia would be really upset if she didn't have it. At every ballet class, she told us about her practices at home. She would have a hard time practicing without her shoes.

I remembered vaguely where Taylor lived, but it had been years since I had been in his neighborhood, so I took the address with me just in case. After a few wrong turns and a couple of U-turns, I eventually made it to his street. The three-story plantation-style house had seemed big before, but now it was simply breathtaking. *I can't imagine living in a house like that! It's like a fairy tale.*

The rumor was that Taylor's mom saw a house for sale in a magazine, then took the picture to an architectural firm and commissioned them to make a house for her that looked exactly like the picture. I wondered how much it had cost. Whatever it was, it was worth it. The front yard looked just like a magical garden, lined with rows and rows of flowers and hedged bushes. Wide, gleaming white steps led to a large front porch that was flanked by six sturdy, carved white pillars.

My plan was to quickly hand over the bag to Mrs. Anderson and then hightail it out of there before Taylor saw me. I parked my mom's Volvo across the street and grabbed the dance bag. After a few breaths to calm my nerves—and a couple of reminders that there was no way Taylor was home and that I was just being chicken—I stepped out of the car and crossed the road.

After passing under the watchful glare of the two fierce lion statues that guarded the home, I hurried up the paved stairs. As I reached the pillars, I paused a moment and looked at the splendor all around me. Never before had I been this close to something so—so, huge. I climbed the last of the steps that led to tall, double French doors adorned with matching floral welcome wreaths.

Another deep shaky breath brought me up to the doorbell. I pushed the white button, then thought, *What if Taylor answers the door? Guess I'll just drop the bag and run.*

I was grateful when the door was answered not by Taylor but by a woman dressed like a maid. "Can I help you, miss?" she asked, giving me an odd look.

I realized I was staring at her. "Oh, sorry. I'm Georgia's ballet teacher, and she left her bag today. Could you give this to her?" I attempted to hand it to the lady, but she had other ideas.

"Oh, Georgia will be so happy to see you." She smiled. "Please come in."

What? No way. "Oh, uh, I would rather—" I was about to protest until the woman opened the door wider and I got a peek inside. The house was incredible. "Oh, okay. Thank you." I smiled as I stepped over the threshold and gawked. *Wow. This is like a movie set.*

I stood for a moment in the large entryway, mesmerized by the gorgeous crystal chandelier before me. Behind it I could just make out the top of a double-sided staircase that cascaded down either side of the marble-floored foyer.

"This way," the woman instructed.

She waited for me to follow her further into the house, but I couldn't. My feet wouldn't budge. All of a sudden I was indescribably nervous. *No thanks,* I wanted to say. *I think I need to go now.* I actually would've dropped the bag and fled the house completely had Taylor not shown up at that precise instant.

"Mrs. Little, was that the doorbell I heard?" his voice came from above me. Dismayed, I froze as I watched his progress down the right set of stairs. First his sock-covered feet, then his jean-clad legs, then his bold-striped chest, then all of him. His steps faltered as he saw me, and our eyes locked.

"Chloe?" he said in obvious disbelief.

He looks so good! I forgot how hot he is, even without shoes. I'm going to melt right here, I thought. Except I couldn't do anything. Speechless and completely paralyzed, I was sure I couldn't have looked like a bigger freak if I tried.

Unfortunately, Taylor had no problem moving as he bounded down the last few stairs.

He's coming. Yikes. In my embarrassment, I looked away from his incredulous stare and saw the ballet bag in my hands. "Oh. Uh, I, this—this is Georgia's," I was able to spit out. "She left it at dance class today." I offered the bag to Taylor as he stopped a few feet away from me, but he wasn't looking at it. My heart jumped.

185

"You're here." His eyes searched my face. "You're actually here."

"Um, yes." I looked away from him, thinking he probably wished I was anywhere else but in his house. I tried to step back and was amazed at my traitorously stubborn feet, which apparently didn't want to be anywhere else. *Breathe. Take a deep breath and breathe.*

"Mrs. Little, I'll take care of Chloe, don't worry," I heard Taylor say near my ear. With a small tug he gently took my hand. My eyes fluttered back to his. *He's holding my hand!*

"Thanks," I heard the woman say as Taylor pulled my hand slowly toward him. I realized then that it was still clamped onto Georgia's bag, and that it was the small tote and not my hand he was really after. I jerked my palm away and released the bag, which fell at Taylor's feet. Mortified, I mumbled, "Sorry," and started to bend over and pick it up.

It was Taylor's hand on my arm that stopped me. "Wait." My eyes fluttered up to his and were held captive by their intensity. Slowly his fingers moved down my arm and left a delicious trail of sparks until his hand held mine again. I gulped, unable to look away. "I'll get the bag," he said.

Then I watched in amazement as he bent over with our hands still clasped, picked up the bag, and stood, in one fluid motion. Thankfully, that action allowed me the moment I needed to collect my wits. "Thank you, Taylor. If you could give that to Georgia for me, I'd be really grateful. Anyway, well, I better go." I would've stepped back but my feet still refused to move. And my hand! My hand refused to even think of pulling out of Taylor's warm hold.

Taylor looked down at our hands and ruefully smiled before he brought them up in between us. Slowly, his thumb traced a small circle on top of mine, whereupon I let out a tiny gasp at the currents that raced up my elbow. His eyes met mine again. After a moment of hesitation, he nodded his head as if deciding on something. "Do you really have to go this second? Come on. I'll take you to see Georgia."

Another slow, lazy circle was drawn over my thumb, but I heard myself answer, "Uh, yeah, of course. I . . . uh" —I could feel my face turning red— "I would love to see Georgia."

"Great." Instantly, Taylor was all smiles. "She's up this way."

He pulled me along after him, and soon we climbed the elegant staircase side by side. As I floated up the stairs, I had visions of attending a royal ball. Of course, in those visions I wasn't wearing jeans and a T-shirt.

"Your house is really big," I remarked, probably sounding like a complete idiot.

"Yeah, I know." He chuckled. "It can get annoying."

"Really?"

"Well, I guess if you like to run then it's not so bad."

"Run?" I couldn't picture anyone running through a house like this.

"Thank goodness we have Mrs. Little. It used to be pretty bad when we were in the back of the house and the doorbell rang. Can you imagine my mom sprinting in her high heels to catch the door? Sometimes we wouldn't even hear the bell ring. People would think we were lying when we said we'd been home all day."

"Wow. I never thought of that."

"Well, that's Mrs. Little's job, really."

"Answering the door?"

"Making sure we don't miss visitors like you." He smiled down at me again and winked.

Wow. He is so hot when he winks.

We walked into a pretty lavender and white room with a huge Victorian-style dollhouse dominating the center. I couldn't see Georgia anywhere.

"Georgia, Miss Chloe's here to see you," Taylor announced.

"What?" the dollhouse answered. Then a mop of golden curls and two happy blue eyes peered around the side. "Miss Chloe! Miss Chloe!" Georgia hollered as she ran around the dollhouse toward me.

"Hi!" I giggled when she almost knocked me over with her energetic hug. Taylor quickly stepped behind me and steadied my shoulders. Georgia's bag in his hand gently bobbed against my arm.

"Sorry. She can get really excited when she sees people she loves," Taylor murmured near my ear.

Loves. The word echoed all around me. Breathlessly, I hugged her back.

"Look what Miss Chloe brought you," Taylor exclaimed. "You left it at the studio today." He brought her tote around so she could see it.

"My ballet bag!" she shouted. "You found-ed it! See, Taylor, I did leave it there!"

"I thought it was in—" Taylor began.

"He thought-ed it was in Mom's car, but it's not. It's here!" Georgia did a giddy little dance. I looked up at Taylor and we both started to laugh.

"Wanna see my dollhouse?" She snatched my hand and began to pull me around to the back of the house.

"Sure," I replied as if I had a choice. "Wow. That is so pretty." I gasped. It was the most beautifully decorated dollhouse I had ever seen. I couldn't help myself. I sat down on the floor next to her.

"Diss is my Barbie," Georgia stated. "Diss one can be yours." She handed me a pretty, redheaded Barbie. "And diss one is Taylor's." She handed it to me, too.

"Taylor's? Are you sure?" I grinned at the dark-haired Ken doll as I turned it over in my hands.

Taylor leaned over the house and smiled down at us. "Yep. That's my Barbie."

I teasingly smirked up at him. "You play with Barbies?"

"Er, yes." Taylor lowered his eyes briefly, then looked at me again. "Just don't tell anyone, okay? I have a reputation to maintain."

I laughed. "Reputation? Believe me, I wouldn't dare repeat this little fact to anyone. They would all think I had gone crazy."

"Well, that's a relief." He laughed too.

"Come on, Taylor," Georgia said. "Me an' Miss Chloe are waitin' for you."

"You are?" Taylor's eyes questioned mine. "Georgia, I think Miss Chloe's very busy. I don't think she can stay and play today."

"Oh. You can't play?" She stared at me pleadingly.

"Well, I can't stay very long. But would it be okay if I played for a few minutes?"

Georgia's face lit up.

I glanced up to see if it was okay with Taylor that I stayed. The look he sent me would've buckled my knees if I'd been standing.

TWENTY-TWO
♥
APRIL'S FOOL

It was just a couple days after I went to Taylor's house that my life nearly fell apart. I remember the day distinctly because it was April Fool's Day. I cannot begin to say how much I wished it was a joke when I received that phone call.

"Hello?"

"Hey, Chloe. This is Taylor."

Taylor? Oh my gosh. He called me. "Hi."

"This is going to sound weird, but could you do me a favor?"

"Um, sure."

"Can you—is there any way you can check on your sister for me?"

"My sister?" *Huh?*

"Yeah, Cassidy. I know it's probably nothing, but I'm—I'm ... okay, look. I pulled up Blake's profile on Facebook because he's been kind of acting funny all week. And I came across something—it may not be any big deal—but could you just check for me and see if she's there at the house?"

"She's here. She's in her room. She went to lie down because she wasn't feeling good."

"You're sure?"

"Yeah, I just talked to her about five minutes ago. So what did Blake's Facebook say? What made you think of Cass?"

"Um—Chloe, this doesn't feel right. Will you check her room, please?"

"Why? I just saw her."

"I would feel a whole lot better if you did. Please?"

Sheez. "All right." I got up off the couch and walked through the kitchen.

"Are you there yet?"

"Hang on." I chuckled as I began to jog down the hallway. "Okay, I'm here. Cass?" I knocked on the door and waited. Taylor's impatient sigh caused me to worry a bit.

"Knock again," he demanded after a couple of seconds.

"Okay, okay." I knocked. "Cassidy? Hey, can you open up?"

"She's not there, is she?"

"Taylor, will you stop. You're beginning to scare me." I tried the handle. It was locked.

"Sorry, I'm just—"

I began to pound on the door. "Cass? Cassidy! Are you asleep? Open the door!" I waited a few more seconds. Nothing. My hand shook as I placed the phone to my other ear. "Taylor, I don't think she's there—"

"Get in that room now! I don't care if you have to break the door down. Get in there. Make sure she's gone."

Frantically, I stood on tiptoe and began to search for the small screwdriver we had above the door. "What happens if she's gone? What does it mean?"

"Don't worry, I'm coming over right now."

192

"Don't you dare hang up, Taylor."

I heard the engine of his sports car roar to life. "Chloe Hart, wanting to stay on the phone with me—imagine that."

"Very funny." I went to my bedroom door and searched above it. "I found the key."

"Is she there?"

"Hang on." My hands were having the hardest time just trying to get the screwdriver in the door handle. *She better be in there. I swear if she isn't, I'll—* The door unlocked. In an instant, I flung the door open and walked into the room. It was empty. Creepily, eerily, empty.

"Chloe?"

I took a breath to calm my nerves before I answered, "She's gone, Taylor."

"Ah, I knew it. Look, I'm about five minutes from your house. I want you to look all around outside, okay? You're sure you talked to her a few minutes ago?"

"Yeah, I'm positive."

"Okay, good. She may still be close by."

I dashed out the back door and ran around to the side of house to Cassidy's bedroom window. It was shut, but I noticed the side gate was open.

"Do you see anything?" Taylor's loud voice in my ear caused me to jump. I had forgotten I was still holding the phone.

"Not out back. I'm going through to the front right now. So are you going to tell me what you saw on Facebook, or what?"

"Or what."

"For crying out loud, you better tell me, Taylor. I have a right to know what your cousin is planning to do to my sister." I rushed to the driveway and looked around. *Where is she?*

"Look, all I saw was that he was planning on meeting some girl somewhere. Most of it was in code on their comments back and forth. I only realized it may be your sister when I saw your profile on her top friends list."

I ran to the end of the street and looked toward my friends' houses. "Holy cow, Taylor. She's fifteen. If he lays one finger on her, I'll—"

"He won't. I promise you that much. And if he does—"

"I don't see her anywhere. I've looked down both sides of the street and nothing. What do I do?" I asked him frantically.

"Hang on. I'll be there in less than two minutes."

I brushed the curls off my face and looked across to the park. "Cassidy!" She was sitting on one of the swings. I started to run across the street and shrieked at the loud, blaring horn of a car. "Ahh!" It careened out of the way, missing me by inches.

Taylor's voice in my ear only confused me more. "Do you see her, Chloe? What's going on? Are you all right? What happened?"

I was so scared, I couldn't answer. With my heart in my throat, I hesitantly looked both ways and walked the rest of the way up to the sidewalk. I glanced back just in time to see Cassidy stand up and look behind her toward the baseball field. My shoes squished in the soft sand as I saw what had caught her attention. "No!" I gasped. I could just make out Blake's blond hair as he came across the grassy field about fifty yards from me.

"Chloe, what—?"

I didn't even answer Taylor as I lowered the phone and ran straight toward Blake. *He is not taking my sister anywhere. Mr. Blake Wilder has messed with the wrong redhead!* All at once everything I had ever felt toward Blake and the ruined relationship I had with Taylor and every other disgusted and mean and scared feeling I had held back, hit me with full force. All I fully remember was a bright flash of red light temporarily blinding me and then *oomph!* I collided into his tall form. "You stay away from her!"

Blake stumbled and we landed with a thud on the soft grass. "W–what?" he gasped.

"Chloe!" Cassidy's shocked cry ricocheted in my ears as she ran up to us.

I jumped to my knees and pointed my finger in his face. "If you so much as touch my sister, you will pay." He crawled away from me on his backside and hands. I had never seen anyone look so genuinely terrified before. It was almost humorous, and he would've gained a bit of mercy from me, but in confusion he lurched into Cassidy's legs. I freaked. "GET AWAY FROM HER NOW!"

I don't know what my face looked like as I sprung up and grabbed Blake's collar, jerking him with me, but he was certainly petrified. "Get up!" I screamed at him while he scrabbled to his feet.

"I—I'm sorry. I'm so sorry," was all he could mutter.

"You will be sorry, you little—!"

"Chloe!"

It was Taylor. He had parked at an angle in the middle of the road and left his car door wide open. As he approached us at a run, I went from raving mad to giddy with joy. "Finally." I smiled as Taylor seized Blake's arms. I was so thankful I would've kissed him if I wasn't holding Blake.

"It's okay, Chloe, I've got him now." I hadn't realized how much larger Taylor was until I saw the two cousins side by side. He gently eased my fingers' vise-like grip on Blake.

"What's wrong, Blake? You look like you've seen a ghost." Taylor shook his head. "Didn't anyone ever tell you rule number one? Don't mess with a redhead."

I glared at Blake. "Or her family."

"Chloe, do me a favor and pull Blake's keys out of his jacket pocket. He isn't going anywhere anytime soon."

My eyes bored into Blake's as I jammed my hands into his jacket pocket. One dimple appeared, and Blake no longer looked afraid. In fact, he looked downright happy that I was this close to him. I thought I was going to hurl.

Blake's eyes smoldered as he smiled at me. "You eighteen yet?"

Taylor lost it. He jerked Blake back from me just as my hands closed around the keys. "You talk to her again and I'll kill you," he growled. "Then I'll let Chloe have what's left."

The fear was back.

I went to hand the keys to Taylor, but he shook his head. "I'll come by later tonight with my dad. I'm sure your parents are going to want to talk to him anyway. One of us will drive this pervert's truck home then."

"Okay."

"Come on, Blake, let's make a trip to the hotel. Dad's there at the moment, and I think he'd like to see you." Taylor jerked on Blake's arms and headed back toward his car. Wisely, Blake remained silent.

And then it hit me. *Cassidy.* I spun around and saw her standing there, her eyes huge. I took a step toward her and she flinched. "What's going on, Chloe? I've never seen you so mad before."

"Are you okay?"

She shakily walked up to me and asked, "Is—is Blake in trouble?"

"Come here." I put my arm around her. "Cass, are you gonna tell me where he said you were going to go?"

"Just to a movie. Honest."

"On a date?" I watched as Taylor loaded Blake into his car. I could tell he was aggravated and barely containing his temper. He walked around the front and waved to us briefly before climbing in.

"Yeah, but I didn't want you to know, because you'd tell Mom. I'm sixteen in like three weeks. It's so not fair I can't date now."

Taylor's car revved to life. Bemused, I watched as the sun glinted off its sleek blue roof before it sped away. Cassidy and I headed back toward the house. "Believe me, Blake is not the type of guy you want to be dating."

"Why? Because you like him?" she defensively asked.

"No. I *did* like him, Cassidy, but I don't now. Blake's not my type." Our feet sunk into the sand as we passed the playground equipment. "Seriously, he's not yours, either. You've got it all wrong. Blake was in court last year for drugging a fifteen-year-old and taking advantage of her."

"No way." Cassidy glanced up.

"Yes." I nodded my head. "I think he was planning to do it again with you. Thank goodness Taylor checked out his Facebook profile and warned me."

"Oh my gosh." Cass stumbled a bit as we headed onto the sidewalk.

"How did he contact you?" I asked.

"He found me on Facebook," she mumbled. "Do you think Mom's going to kill me?"

I chuckled. "Probably." We crossed the street, this time checking for traffic.

"You think it's going to be bad, then?"

"Ah, nothing more than your typical 'grounded for life.'"

Cass moaned.

I squeezed her shoulder as we started up the driveway. "Hey, no matter what happens, I'm just grateful you're safe."

She sighed. "How much do you think we owe Taylor?"

Everything. No matter how much he will try to deny it, Taylor Anderson truly is a superhero.

TWENTY-THREE

♥

RANDOM RUMOR

So you want to know what's worse than being up half the night talking to the Andersons, your parents, *and* the media? Yep, someone at the hotel leaked the story to the press. You'll never guess, so I'll tell you. It was going to school Friday morning— dead tired and fully exhausted, walking around like a zombie— and overhearing that Taylor had a date to prom. Not that it mattered, because it didn't. I mean, duh, he's Taylor Anderson, right? So why should it bother anyone at all that he had a date? I mean seriously, there is no one who would care less than me.

Except that's what I didn't get. I did care! What was I thinking, anyway—that he'd miraculously start loving me again because he saved my sister? *Yeah, right.* He was probably more disgusted with us than anything. I mean, hello? Better stay away from the Hart sisters—talk about trouble. One's got a temper and will rip your head off for crossing her, and the other is so flirtatious she'll start dating anyone she meets on the internet.

So it's obvious, I decided. *I will never see Taylor again. I get it. I blew it. And really, it is a good thing. Because who wants to be popular anyway? It's so highly overrated, it's a joke. I certainly don't want to be. I don't, really. I just want the guy* behind *the popularity.*

I stopped walking to my art class as the reality of that last thought hit me. I had just admitted to myself that I liked Taylor Anderson, and I was flabbergasted. *Oh my gosh. How much more blinded by fear and pride could I have been?* I was totally afraid to have my heart broken by another popular jerk, and too proud to see that there was actually a different Taylor Anderson—a real, sweet, caring Taylor Anderson beneath all the popularity. I finally realized I actually preferred the guy *behind* what everyone else saw.

And to think he used to love me. Me.

"Hey, Chloe."

I turned to see Madison jogging to catch up. "Yeah?" I half smiled and began to walk again as she joined me.

"Wow, so I heard about Blake. How are you doing? Why didn't you say anything?"

I guess now would be a good time to point out that the school had also been talking about Cassidy and Blake. Not that I blame them. I mean, it made the 10:00 news last night and the local newspaper this morning. It was such a hot story that it almost trumped Taylor asking a girl to prom. Almost.

I shrugged at Madison. "There comes a point when you have talked to so many reporters that you get tired of talking about it, you know? I figured most people know anyway."

"Well, how's Cassidy? Is she okay?"

"Yeah, she woke up with a raging fever this morning. I think the stress of last night might've added to everything. I mean it's pretty embarrassing to have strangers and your parents go through all of your Facebook messages, phone texts, and emails, especially when you have to answer questions about every one. Cass was up later than I was, and I went to bed way after midnight. But I think she'll be okay—much better than she could've been."

"Yeah. That Blake guy is a creep," Madison said. "Thank goodness for Taylor."

I owed so much to Taylor. My whole family did. Who knew that his feeling he should check out Blake's Facebook profile would lead to my sister being saved?

Walking on in silence, I contemplated the "almost"s and "could have been"s that surrounded Cassidy's ordeal yesterday.

Madison interrupted my thoughts. "Hey, I've got some news that'll cheer you up."

"You do? What is it?"

"Guess who got nominated for prom king?" she practically gushed.

"Uh, Taylor?" I snorted.

"Well, yeah, but who else?"

"Oh, um, Zack?" I tried.

"Okay. Yes, but who else? Come on Chloe, think. Who is the least likely to be nominated for prom king, but would make the coolest king ever?"

Is this some sort of trick question? "Okay, who would I never think of? Uh, I don't know. I give up."

"Ethan. Ethan's been nominated for prom king." She began to jump up and down.

Ethan? Ethan! "Shut up. Ethan got nominated for prom king? Eeeh. That is so cool!" I jumped with her.

"Voting starts Monday, so don't forget, okay?" she said as we joined Alyssa for art.

Maybe life isn't so bad after all, I thought. *I mean. Alyssa got Zack, who she deserves. Madison loves Collin and is so happy to have a boyfriend. My sister is safe. And Ethan just got nominated for prom king. Life is good. Plus my birthday's in fourteen days. I'll finally be an adult. That's just weird and cool all at the same time.*

Suddenly, I wondered if Ethan had a date to prom. He would be way fun to go with.

A couple of days later I got an email from Ethan. I thought it might've been a casual invite to prom now that he had been nominated for king. And I was right to an extent—it was a prom invite, just not for me. Cassidy was grounded from all media outlets, like the phone, email, Facebook, etc., so it would make sense that Ethan would email me to ask her for him. The lucky girl! Her birthday was actually the night of prom, so I was positive my parents would relent and let her go, just this once. Plus there was the added fact that they adored Ethan.

Needless to say Cassidy was all smiles, bragging, and giddy giggles. She was so happy about Ethan asking her to prom that I really couldn't be too jealous or sad. With all of the gossip that was going around school about her, she needed to feel special. It took three days of begging but my parents finally agreed to let her go. I think what closed the deal for them was that Cassidy was able to borrow a dress from one of her friends. So with the security of not having to buy an extra dress this year, Cass was free to go. Thank goodness no one commented on my peculiar lack of a date. I don't think I could've handled it.

Me not having a date didn't stop rumors from flying. It was eight days before prom—and exactly one day before my birthday. Imagine my surprise when I saw Kylie sitting in her car in front of my house as I pulled into the driveway after ballet. *What is she doing here?*

I got out of the Volvo, grabbed my gear, and headed over to Kylie's car to see if she needed something. By the time I had made it halfway down the driveway, she was heading up. She looked totally bent—completely ticked off—so I decided to stand my ground and wait for her. From the look on her face, this would not be a sweet little chat. *What gives?* I noticed she was wearing her cheerleading workout clothes.

"Hi, Kylie." I smiled. *Maybe I can kill her with kindness.*

She got right to the point. "Look, we need to talk." Then she smiled her beauty queen smile at me.

"Great." My smile got wider. "Would you like to go inside?"

Kylie looked up at the house and sneered.

Careful, dear, someone might see your true character.

Then she turned back to me, her smile in place. "No thank you. Out here is fine." She pointed to my front lawn. "I don't plan on being here that long anyway."

"Fine." I walked over to my mom's bench and dropped my ballet bag on it. When I'd turned around, Kylie had followed. "So what do you want?" I placed my hands on my hips.

"I want you to stop this lie that you've been spreading around, that's what." She flipped her hair over her shoulder.

I expected Kylie to elaborate, but she didn't, so I finally asked, "What lie? What are you talking about?" All pretense of a smile was gone from her face.

Kylie looked like she was going to freak out. "What do you mean what lie? You know perfectly well what I'm talking about. Don't try and play stupid with me."

I blinked. There was no way I was getting into it with her. She better explain herself quickly or I was out of there. Nothing ticked me off more than cheerleaders who thought they were better than everyone, and I refused to play her game.

"The lie about you and Taylor going to prom together! I know you made it up. I know you're just—"

"What in the—? What are you talking about?"

"You've been telling everyone you're going with him, so that way Taylor will feel like he has to take you. Well, it's not going to work. Taylor's taking me to prom."

I started to laugh. It was unbelievable. *This is why she left her cheerleading practice early to come to my house? Because of a rumor? Figures.* I turned around, swept up my bag on my shoulder, and then faced her. "Don't believe everything you hear, Kylie."

"Are you telling me you're not going to prom with Taylor?" She took a step forward.

"Look, if you're going with him to prom, congratulations. It's obvious I'm not, isn't it?" *Why is she still here?*

She looked confused.

Good. That makes two of us. I folded my arms.

"But has he asked you?"

I grinned. "Has who asked me what?"

Kylie lost it. "Taylor. Has Taylor Anderson asked you to prom?"

"You just told me he asked you, and you just told me I was lying about him asking me. So if he has already asked you to prom and you're certain I'm lying, then why are you here, Kylie?"

"Ooh!" Kylie took a deep breath. "Look, Taylor and I have promised to go to senior prom together ever since we were in grade school, and I'm not going to let anyone mess it up for me, especially you. Do you have any idea how long I have planned for this day? My dress, my shoes, my nails, my hair, all planned months in advance. Not only will you be hurting me, but you'll completely trash any chances you ever had of becoming popular.

It's bad enough I have to watch Zack make a fool over himself with Alyssa, but believe me, if you come within twenty feet of Taylor, I'll make sure everyone hates you!" Her voice rang with triumph.

Promises, promises. "Ooh, I'm so sad. What would I ever do if Kylie and her friends never talked to me again?"

"I could make your life miserable."

"Do me a favor and get out of my yard, now." I didn't even give her the courtesy of pointing.

"Not until you promise me that you won't go to prom with Taylor."

I shook my head at her immaturity and shrugged. "Fine, then stay. But I don't have to promise you anything. I can do whatever I want." I hitched my bag, brushed past her, and headed toward the door.

"Chloe, if you walk in that house without promising to stay away from Taylor, I'll go to him myself and make sure he stays away from you."

I slammed the door behind me as I stormed into the house. After a few seconds, I heard Kylie's tires screech as she peeled out of our street.

What I have I done? What in the world is she going to tell Taylor?

TWENTY-FOUR
♥
BIRTHDAY WISH

The next day was Friday, my birthday. I managed to keep my head down the whole day and keep out of earshot of everyone. I didn't need to know I was being talked about. I would much rather live in a bubble and believe everything was all right than to see the world as it fell in around me.

As my last birthday in high school, it didn't go so well. Alyssa and Madison both forgot it was my birthday. I had specifically steered away any conversation about this day for the last two weeks, since I didn't want them to change their plans with their boyfriends for me. They had planned a double date to go bowling. Maybe if we all had guys it wouldn't have been so bad, but I really didn't want to be pitied or be the third wheel.

So, on Friday night, I found myself celebrating my birthday alone. Dad and Mom had planned to go to a double feature at the movie theater, and Cass and Claire were spending the night at friends' houses. Mom was so sweet—she had even gone and bought a small ice cream cake for Alyssa, Madison, and I to devour. It was my favorite, an expensive Oreo cookies 'n' cream cake from Baskin Robbins. I stared at the cake Mom had left on the counter to soften and knew I'd have to at least eat some of it or she would know what had happened. I got a knife from the butcher's block and even attempted to cut the thing before I gave up. I wrapped the whole cake back in its packaging and placed it in the freezer for later. I just didn't have the heart yet to eat my birthday cake all by myself.

This is my eighteenth birthday—I'm finally an adult. There is no reason to feel sad. None at all. I have wonderful friends who are happier than they've ever been before. I have a happy family that loves me. I even have happy ballet students. Happy people and happiness are all around me. So what's the big deal? This should be a very happy birthday for me. Pluck up! Besides, it's not like eighteen is all that special anyway. I mean, there are plenty of other ages out there that are just as fun like, seventeen and nineteen and . . .

I had just planned to go ahead and let the first tear fall when the doorbell rang. I wasn't exactly dressed for company. I mean, I still had my ballet clothes on under my jeans, and my hair was up in a poufy ponytail. Thank goodness I hadn't started crying yet! Heavens knows I'm not pretty when I cry. After a couple of tugs at my shirt, I shrugged my shoulders and answered the door.

There stood Taylor Anderson. His dark hair was slightly tousled, his chest was moving at the rapid pace of his breathing, and his blue eyes smoldered into mine. My heart flip-flopped. It would've done more but it didn't have a chance. Without saying a word Taylor crossed over the threshold, took me in his arms, and kissed me. I was shocked, dazed, and a little breathless. He grinned at my discomposure when he released me slightly, just long enough to whisper in my ear, "That was for being the only girl I've ever known that would stand up to Kylie. And this—" he brought me close again and kissed me a second time "—was for handling Blake. And this—this is for you."

My heart literally stopped beating when I realized he would kiss me again. In an instant my lashes fluttered closed. I felt two gentle fingers tilt my chin up just before his mouth captured mine. The kiss nearly caused me to dissolve into a puddle. Taylor chuckled as he held me tighter to keep me from falling before he continued to kiss me again in the softest, gentlest, most romantic kiss a girl could ever wish for.

When he released me, I thought my insides had turned to jelly. I braced myself on one side of the doorframe and breathed, really breathed for the first time since he had arrived. Taylor chuckled again and braced himself on the other side of the doorframe with the front door still wide open. I relished the cool breeze on my warm skin and glanced up at him. He looked almost as stunned as I did.

Our eyes met and he smiled. "Wow, girl, you can really pack a punch." He shook his head. "I don't think my heart has ever beat that fast."

"Mine actually stopped," I admitted. We were too close—way too close. I couldn't stop my eyes from shining into his.

"Well, I promise I won't move," Taylor said. "Go ahead then. I'm waiting."

"Go ahead?" *Am I supposed to kiss him again?*

"You know, slap me. I know you would've had I given you the chance. So go ahead. I'm all yours."

He's all mine. "You want me to slap you?" I couldn't help smiling—he looked so amazingly attractive staring down at me.

"I know I should apologize. You're probably expecting me to. But I'm not—"

"Taylor Darcy Anderson, if you dare try to apologize for kissing me, I *will* slap you." I placed my hands on my hips.

"Are you serious?" His eyes began to glitter into my own.

Okay, is there a hotter guy in the world?

"What?" Taylor matched my smile. "What are you smiling about?"

"So is that why you came over?" I asked.

"To kiss you?" He grinned impishly. "Well, yeah. I'd wanted to for so long. And then—and then, when Kylie came over and said all she did, I couldn't help myself. I drove straight here. My only thought was to kiss you senseless."

"Really? You mean she didn't tell you about it yesterday?"

"No, I was gone yesterday. Today was the first time I'd seen her. Why?"

"So you came to kiss me senseless?" I decided to get back to the good part.

"Yeah, I figured I'd pay for it later."

"Oh, you'll pay," I teased. "Don't think you can get off that easy." I stepped back and rested my hand on the door handle.

"Seriously, Chloe, I . . . I can't, I can't—" Taylor took a deep breath and steadied himself a moment before he continued on. "I can't take this any longer. I still love you. If you want me, then the offer stands. If not, I—I promise I'll never bring it up again."

Slowly, I stepped toward the doorframe. I placed one hand on his chest—which he immediately covered with his own—and I wound the other up his shoulder and around his neck. I could feel the frantic beating of his heart as I stood on tiptoe and gently lowered his cheek to my lips, and then mischievously whispered, "Only if you take me to prom."

"Done." He chuckled and held me in place when I went to pull away. "Are you sure you want to go to prom with me? Sure, I can dance, but not anything like what you're used to."

"Don't worry about that." I laughed and rested my cheek against his chest. It felt so good to be in his arms. "I'm a dance teacher, remember?"

Taylor laughed and held me tighter. "Hey, do you want to go out to dinner or something? Movie?"

I looked up. "Yes. But I, uh—I can't."

"Why? Are you watching your sister or something?"

"Nope. I have the place entirely to myself."

"Oh, so are you grounded?" he teased.

I laughed. "No. It's just that you haven't passed the Dating Ritual yet. My parents would so have a heart attack if they found out I went out with someone they haven't tested. And uh, I don't know if you grasp just how much of a high-profile celebrity you are around here. Someone is bound to talk."

He laughed. "So I guess coming in is out of the question, too?"

"Well, from the looks of Ms. Jenkins's curtains next door, I'm going to say yes. She's probably already had an eyeful the way you kissed me with the door wide open. Oh my gosh! I wonder how many people saw us." I looked up at him.

"Not enough. I want everyone to know you're mine."

Eeeh! I'm Taylor Anderson's. I can't believe it. I began to giggle. I knew I was totally acting like all of the other girls, but I didn't care. And I have to say, it was really good to be thought of as his.

"Okay, then, how about the park?" he said. "It's not a date, right? And we won't be in the house alone with Ms. Jenkins's dirty mind inventing stuff. What do ya say?"

"Actually, yeah. Let's go to the park. Hang on." I ran into the kitchen and got the house key, then grabbed the ice cream cake and slipped a couple of spoons into my pocket.

"What's that?" Taylor asked as he shut the door behind us.

I locked the door. "Oh, just a silly cake my mom bought for me."

Taylor pulled the package out of my arms. "Really? And that's why it says 'Happy Birthday' on it?"

Dang. "What?" I leaned over his arm and looked through the cellophane top. "Sheez."

Taylor chuckled and wrapped his arm around my shoulders, his other hand clutching the cake. I turned and waved at Ms. Jenkins's window and watched the curtain fall. Taylor and I waited for a couple of cars to pass before we headed across the street. My feet began to sink into the soft sand.

"You know, I've never thanked you for what you've done for Georgia."

"Georgia?" I grinned as we made our way over to the swings.

"I don't know if you knew this, but Georgia used to be really shy."

I pulled away a little to see him. "Georgia? Shy?"

Taylor stopped about three feet from the swings. "Yes. She was really shy. We were actually worried about it. She was so afraid of people that she would hardly even talk to anyone outside of the family. If she hadn't improved when she did, my parents would've been forced to hold her back from attending kindergarten next school year. Georgia's therapist recommended that she try ballet. It was really a last-ditch effort on my parents' part to see if she would improve.

"She did, almost immediately. All it took was watching you dance. And she loved you. You were like a storybook ballerina come to life. I couldn't help but spoil her when she wanted to bring something to your class. It was the first time we had ever seen her share with anyone besides us before. My mom cried the first day she overheard Georgia chatter about her new friends. Up until ballet, all the friends Georgia would ever talk to or about were her dolls. My parents and I owe you so much."

I stepped away from him. "Taylor, I had no idea, none at all. I honestly thought Georgia was one of the most outgoing little girls I had ever met." I laughed quietly to myself. "I've had a hard time getting her to be quiet long enough to teach the next move or step to her. She is such a sweetheart." I paused a moment. "Which reminds me, since we are on the subject of sisters, I have a not quite-so-sweetheart sister I need to thank you for."

"Me? All I did was follow a hunch to check Blake's Facebook profile. I freaked out when I saw that Cassidy had left a comment saying she planned on meeting Blake that day."

"You were freaked? You have no idea how disturbed I was when he showed up for my sister. I lost it. Seriously, I have never been so mad in my entire life. I don't know what I would've done to the loser if you hadn't shown up when you did. It would probably have been me in jail and him off for self-defense—if he lived."

Taylor laughed and opened his arms wide, cake and all. "That's my girl."

His girl. I stepped back into his arms again, knowing I could cheerfully be held by him all day long.

"So when were you going to tell me it was your birthday?" Taylor playfully nudged me.

I smiled into his shirt. "Oh, I don't know. I was going to wait and see if you were worthy enough to know. Maybe in about six months."

"Six months, huh? That's too bad."

I pulled back. "What do you mean?"

"I guess you don't want the present I got you, then."

213

"What? You got me a present?" My jaw dropped. "No, you didn't. You're just giving me a hard time. Besides, you wouldn't have. You thought I was going to slap you earlier."

"True. False. And true. I didn't, really. It was supposed to be a Valentine's present. I got it around Christmastime."

"You're kidding me." *Taylor got me a present back in December?*

"Nope. Here." He set the cake on the ground and then put his hand in his pocket. "You've gotta close your eyes, okay?"

"Fine." A bit skeptical, I agreed and closed my eyes. I felt Taylor's hand as it slid down my forearm and clasped mine.

He chuckled as he tried to pry my fingers open. "It won't bite, I promise."

I grinned and reluctantly allowed my hand to release. Taylor placed something on my palm. It felt like soft fabric with a hard object wrapped inside.

"Okay, you can open them now."

It was a velvet drawstring bag. I looked up at Taylor, then opened the bag and pulled out a really pretty charm bracelet. "Wow! I've always wanted one of these." I watched as it glistened and sparkled in the setting sun.

"Do you like it? Each charm represents something." He leaned over me. "See, this one is a heart, because every time I see a heart I think of you. My Chloe Hart. This is a basketball, because that was what I was playing when I first fell for you. Oh! Here's a little mask for all of the Halloween parties you host. Here's a paintbrush and palette to represent art class. Here's a Bible, because I know how much you love church, and here's—"

I couldn't help it. I turned and stopped him with a kiss. I had no idea he knew me as well as he did, or remembered all of those things. It was the most thoughtful gift I had ever been given. "Thank you, Taylor. Really, thank you."

"So you like it?"

"Are you kidding? This is the best gift anyone has ever given me." *Seriously, is there a sweeter guy in the world?*

TWENTY-FIVE
♥
PROM

"Chloe, you look incredible," Cassidy exclaimed as she walked into my room. Kate had just zipped up my new prom dress. I had told my parents not to worry about buying me a new one—I would just wear my old one from last year. But my dad wouldn't hear of it. He was adamant that no daughter of his would wear a used dress when she was going on the arm of an Anderson.

"Thanks. I feel incredible." I smiled as I glanced down at my dark bluish green iridescent gown. The skirt swept out like a princess with multicolored layers of sparkly tulle. In the mirror, I watched my hands as they fingered the smooth sequins that were stitched in a band around my waist, my new charm bracelet sparkling in the mirror. I liked the way the bodice had gathers of tulle that connected to a small band of more sequins that formed the neckline. But my favorite part was the wispy, glittering fairy sleeves that fell daintily over my shoulders and slightly down my arms. Unconsciously, my hand traveled up to play with one of the darker blue wisps of a sleeve. I was so glad my dad convinced me to get the dress. My old dress was pretty, but nowhere near as gorgeous as this one. I spun around so I could admire all of me in the mirror.

Kate sighed. "You do look elegant."

"Thanks to your talent with hair. This updo is so awesome." I giggled and watched in the mirror as couple of long, red tendrils brushed against my back.

"Okay, so come on, you two. What do you think of my dress?" Cassidy twirled in front of the door.

"Very pretty," Kate said.

I smiled at my sister. "Wow. It fits perfectly. I love the pink color, too. You make the perfect birthday girl."

"Well, of course no one is going to outshine you tonight. But I guess I can accept that fact." Cassidy grinned and put her arm around my shoulders. "I mean how cool is this? My sister is going to prom with *the* Taylor Anderson. I still can't get over it. Just remember me when you're famous, okay?"

"Oh, please." Embarrassed, I shrugged her arm off my shoulders. "What am I going to be famous for? Writing a memoir about my boyfriend?"

"There's an idea!" She laughed. "I know a ton of girls who would love to read it. Heck, I would. Just think, we can all live vicariously through you."

I shook my head and slipped my feet into my new crystal-studded silver sandals.

"And if you put details of his kisses in there, you'll be sure to sell out."

"That is one thing that will never be in any book." I lifted a secretive eyebrow in my mirror at Cassidy. "I think Taylor's kisses are definitely something no writing could do justice to. And—" I cut in before Cass could protest "—that's all I'm going to say about it." I caught Kate's grin in the mirror and turned.

"Thank you! Thank you! Thank you!" I squeezed her. "I don't know what I would've done without you. Twice now you've made me so gorgeous I didn't even recognize myself."

"You're welcome," she gasped, then giggled as she pulled herself out of my overenthusiastic hug. "I wouldn't have it any other way. I'm just glad it all worked out for you. Holy cow, I'm at least five years older than Taylor, and even I'd have gone with him had he asked. There is something very charismatic about him, don't you think?"

"Chloe! Cassidy!" My dad hollered down the hallway. "We're done. You girls can come in and get photos now."

Finally. I wasn't sure if Taylor would actually survive the Dating Ritual. I mean, I had prepped him about being funny, but you never knew what my parents would come up with. Earlier my dad had been cleaning a shotgun he'd borrowed from a guy at work, so I was pretty worried.

I walked behind Cassidy into the family room and saw Taylor there waiting for me. One glance in his eyes and I knew he was mine forever.

Cassidy moved over to Ethan's side—he'd just gone through the ritual for her—allowing Taylor to get his first full glimpse of me. His mouth fell open, which I swear is the ultimate compliment. Within two strides he was at my side, his arm wrapped possessively around my shoulders.

After a surreptitious look around the room, he leaned over and whispered in my ear, "Chloe Elizabeth Hart, you are the most beautiful girl I have ever seen."

He called me beautiful! I looked up through my eyelashes at him and asked, "Ever? Are you sure—?" I would've teased him more but just then his intense gaze nearly took my breath away.

"Don't look at me like that," he said breathlessly. "I don't care who's watching, I'll kiss you speechless."

"You couldn't kiss me speechless if you tried," I teased back, staring at him through my eyelashes again.

Taylor chuckled and half groaned before pulling me closer in front of him for the pictures. "Smile. And stop looking so—so tempting."

"Tempting, hmm?" I smiled happily. Flirting with Taylor was so much fun, and I couldn't wait to spend a million hours teasing him. *One thing is for certain . . .*

"One thing is for certain—" Taylor echoed my thoughts in my ear "—it will never be boring, will it? You never cease to amaze me, Chloe Hart. And I don't think you ever will."

"Oh, I hope not. Taylor Anderson. Your reactions are far too priceless."

"Smile," he gritted through his teeth.

I smiled.

Later at the prom, everyone gasped as Taylor and I entered the building. Not that they didn't know about us already—it was just the first time most of them had actually seen us together. We danced every song, and I have to say Taylor was a pretty good dancer. He definitely didn't have two left feet, that's for sure.

Halfway through the night, they announced the prom king and queen. My heart leapt for joy when Ethan's name was called out as king. I think the whole room went deathly silent before we all broke into applause. I have never seen such a look of shock and terror on anyone's face as I did on Ethan's. Cassidy had to practically push him the whole way to the podium. Even then I don't think he wanted the crown until Taylor—his first attendant—put it on him. Zack was his second attendant. It was the coolest moment to see Taylor, Ethan, and Zack up there on the podium together.

I watched a little jealously as Taylor led the first attendant to the queen out on the floor for the royalty dance. The girl stared right at him the whole time, but Taylor's eyes rarely left mine, so my jealousy didn't last long.

After the honor dance was over, I saw Taylor walk over to the deejay—who totally rocked—and ask him something. Taylor was given the thumbs up for whatever it was. Then he smiled and nodded as he accepted a microphone.

Oh my gosh. What is he going to do?

"This next song is for the most beautiful girl I know." The room stopped at the sound of Taylor's voice, and then everyone turned and stared at me.

He is so dead.

"With Chloe Hart's permission, I would like to dedicate this song to her and the three—almost four—years I had to wait for her to be mine. This is for you." He pointed right at me.

Maybe I could kill him twice.

And then the deejay started playing the song "So Close" from the movie *Enchanted.* Taylor walked over to me and chuckled. "If looks could kill, I'd be dead." In one swift movement, he took me in his arms and we were waltzing—in front of the whole prom! *What is it with waltzing with a guy and your heart melting on the spot? All Taylor has to do is hold me close and I am lost.*

The haunting lyrics took over my mind, as they always do when I listen to that song. It really did fit us. I closed my eyes a moment and allowed him to dip and sway and twirl me across the floor. We slowed a bit as the song slowed, and I rested my cheek on his shoulder. In Taylor's strong, gentle arms, I felt incredibly cherished and protected. I knew then what I had been hesitant all along to believe, and it was time to share it with Taylor. So I stood on my tiptoes and allowed my mouth to brush against his ear as I whispered, "I love you."

He stopped, right in the middle of the floor with everyone watching. "Really?"

I grinned and nodded and pulled his mouth down to my own. And then he did it. Taylor Anderson kissed me speechless.

For the rest of the night we mingled mostly with Collin, Madison, Zack, Alyssa, Ethan, and Cass in between songs. Madison and Alyssa looked amazing, by the way. Maddi was in a gorgeous white dress that was slim and hugged her figure until it flared out at the bottom. Seriously, she looked like a movie star. And Alyssa's dress was soft blue, as beautiful and feminine as any dress I had ever seen. She even wore a small tiara in her hair. Honestly, she looked just like a princess.

I don't think either of my friends—or I, for that matter—had ever received so many compliments in one day before. We were instant celebrities. Madison and Alyssa handled it like pros. But none of us enjoyed the attention as much as Collin did. For my part, I decided it wasn't so bad. I mean, a little bit of me really liked to hear the gossip that surrounded Taylor and me, but only because I knew who the real Taylor was. And he was mine.

I slipped my arm around his waist next to me as he chatted to some of his adoring fans. I felt his arm slide possessively around my shoulders, and I rested my head contentedly against the side of his chest.

I wonder if Kylie Russell is here? I thought suddenly. I would've stood on my tiptoes to search for her, but then I found I didn't care enough to break Taylor's hold on me. In the end, I guess I wasn't too surprised to learn it was Kylie behind the phone calls that broke up Taylor's relationship with Anne at the beginning of the year. Anyone could see Kylie was obsessed with the guy. When Taylor told me she had admitted to calling Anne—which Kylie confessed to in a last-ditch effort to keep him—it was Anne I really felt sorry for. She obviously didn't know Taylor any better than I did at the time.

I had often wondered lately how many girls who had gone out with him had ever actually *seen* Taylor. I mean, sure they saw the guy with the killer smile, the guy who had a nice sports car and a totally awesome house. And I'm positive they relished the status that followed him wherever he went. But did any of those girls really see the guy underneath all of that, the Taylor that loved his family and community and helped people all around him?

"Hey, beautiful." Taylor kissed the top of my curls.

"Hmm?" I lifted my head a bit and peeked up at him.

"I have something for you."

I didn't think I would ever get used to his gorgeous eyes. "You do?"

Taylor grinned. "Well, its two things, actually."

"Two?" I pulled a bit away from him. "Taylor, are you kidding me?"

He chuckled. "Nope. Come on, I'll show you." Taylor tugged on my hand and pulled me through a door that led outside and away from onlookers.

I giggled. "Taylor, I swear if you've bought me something else. I'm gonna—"

"You're gonna what?" he challenged.

"I'm—uh . . . I'll think of something," I finished lamely.

"Well, to ease your mind, it's nothing big. But the other thing I have for you is some news."

"News?"

"I'll tell you in a minute. First, I wanted to add this to your charm bracelet."

I gasped as Taylor pulled out the most adorable miniature silver ballet slippers from his tuxedo jacket pocket. "Oh, Taylor! They're perfect. Thank you."

He held up my hand and began to fasten the slippers to the chain. "It wouldn't have been a perfect charm bracelet without your dancing shoes, especially now that you've been accepted to Arizona State University."

"Well, thanks to Ms. Chavez. I owe her so much." I smiled and dangled the charms. I loved the clinking sound they made when they touched each other. It sounded like quiet little bells.

"Which leads me to my news," Taylor said.

"Oh? My ballet dancing has led you to news?" I teased.

His eyes twinkled in the moonlight. "Actually, it has. Well, I didn't tell anyone until I knew for certain, but about three months ago I applied for a school in Tempe."

"Tempe? As in Arizona?" My head jerked up.

"I found out there was this amazing specialty graphic design school in Tempe called Collins College. Anyway, I didn't want to say anything to you just in case I didn't make it. But I got the acceptance letter this afternoon, and I am so in."

"Are you kidding me?" My jaw dropped.

"Uh, nope. You're not getting rid of me that easily."

"Taylor! We're going to be living in the same city!" I squealed and threw my arms around him.

"And the best part is our campuses are only two and a half miles away from each other."

"No way." I laughed. "We could walk if we wanted to."

"When you didn't buy my fan-club nonsense all those years ago, I knew you were unique. I'm completely serious when I say I fell in love with you right then, because I knew if you ever loved me, it would be because you loved me for who I am and not what I am."

"I love you, Taylor." I smiled. "I love you, I love you, I love you!" By the second "I love you," Taylor had me scooped back in his arms.

Don't you think life is funny sometimes? For almost four years, I dodged the perfect guy. Little did I imagine he had been waiting for me all along. That's why I just had to tell the story of Taylor Anderson and the year I finally came to my senses, got over my silly pride, and fell in love!

ABOUT THE AUTHOR

♥

Jenni James is a busy mom of seven children who is married to a totally hot Air Force recruiter. When she isn't busy chasing her kids around the house, she's dreaming of new romantic books to write. *Pride & Popularity* is the first book in Jenni's series, The Jane Austen Diaries. The second book in the series, *Northanger Alibi,* will be released by Inkberry Press in November 2011.

To find out more about The Jane Austen Diaries or Jenni's other projects, please visit her website, authorjennijames. com, or her Facebook page, The Jane Austen Diaries. Jenni loves to hear from her readers and may be contacted at jenni@ authorjennijames.com.

For a sneak peek at *Northanger Alibi,*

the next book in The Jane Austen Diaries,

just turn the page!

NORTHANGER ALIBI

♥

CHAPTER 1

"Are you kidding?" I gasped as I bounced on my family's multicolored striped couch. "You want to take me? Me? To Seattle? Are you sure?"

"Yep." The older woman across from me grinned. "That is, if your parents say you can go." She smiled the sweetest smile I'd ever seen toward my mom and dad, who were perched nervously on the matching loveseat.

"Please, Mom?"

I couldn't believe one of my mom's best friends just asked me to go with her and her husband on his business trip this summer—to Seattle, of all places! Seattle was only my favorite dreamiest vacation spot ever.

"You really want Claire to come with you?" Mom asked, clearly hedging. She had that deer-in-the-headlights look on her face—you know, the one that reads, "Dang. Now what am I going to do?" She knew Washington was my favorite state and that I would totally give my right arm to go. I had only whined and pleaded every day for the last three years for my parents to take us on a road trip up there.

My mom's problem was letting her baby go. And why she still considered me her baby, I'll never know.

"Are you sure you wouldn't be happier taking Cassidy?" she asked Darlene.

Cass? Are you kidding me? "Mo–om." *What planet of Totally Unfair did she come from, anyway?*

Darlene shook her head. "Actually, I was really hoping for a younger girl, since the president of Seattle's Northwest Academy—where most of the meetings will be held—has a couple of children in high school. Cassidy is older than that, right? I promised them the next time I came, I'd bring children their age."

Two things in that little speech stuck out at me—two things I'm sure were meant to excite me but that somehow dampened my whole outlook on the trip: "children" and "promised to bring children."

Ugh. Are the kids so ugly and weird that Darlene has to bring friends with her so they'll have someone to hang out with?

Yeah, that didn't sit well with me. But surprisingly, it seemed to perk Mom up. "Oh, so there'll be another family there with children Claire's age?" she asked. "She'll have friends?"

"Oh, yes," Darlene said. "They will be so grateful to have her there, you have no idea. They are practically desperate for friends."

"D–desperate for f–friends?" *Um, can we say warning flag, anyone? Great. If they're that worried about having friends, maybe this whole going-to-Seattle-thing wasn't the greatest idea after all . . .*

"And you'll be gone for . . . how long?" Mom really must've

been warming up to the idea.

Darlene shrugged and smiled. "I don't know. It all depends on how quickly Roger can pick up the training he needs. It could take anywhere from three to four weeks all the way up to eleven or twelve weeks. Claire could be in Washington the whole summer."

The whole summer? Never mind the weirdo high-school-age children. I am so going! A whole summer in Seattle is worth enduring anything—anything at all.

"Wow! The whole summer?" Mom gasped. "That's a long time. What do you think, Dave?" My mom turned a bit to study my dad's face, which was a massively good sign. She only asked my dad his opinion if she wasn't willing to say no herself, and the chances of my dad saying no were slim.

"I think we should let her go." He smiled over at me, and my heart soared. "Who knows when another opportunity like this will come around?"

Yes!

"Did you know Washington is one of the places Claire has always wished she could go?" my dad asked Darlene.

"Really? Isn't this your lucky day then? When I was a girl, I always wanted to visit somewhere exotic, like Hawaii. I'll never forget the moment I learned my husband had arranged our honeymoon there." She leaned back and laughed softly. "Oh, I shrieked and shrieked and danced around the room. My poor fiancé didn't know what to do with me." She glanced back over at my parents. "I'll bring Roger over later. Maybe we'll treat you guys to dinner or something—we'll see. But I promise we'll definitely get together so we can work out the details. I hope you know you can completely trust us."

"Oh, no. I'm not worried, honestly," Mom said. "I would trust you with anyone. It's just I'm not used to being away from

Claire that long."

Oh, brother. I rolled my eyes and willed myself not to freak out about her extremely overprotective nature. *As if I would ever do anything wrong. We're talking me here, the good daughter.* My mind wandered back a few years to the day my sister Cassidy nearly caused my parents to have heart attacks when she agreed to meet this crazy guy in secret. Thank goodness our older sister Chloe and her boyfriend Taylor found her in time. In that moment, life at the Hart house changed, and my mom has been completely over-the-top protective of us ever since. It's like she never trusts us anymore. Not that I blame her. I mean, we all thought Blake was pretty cool until he tried to disappear with Cass. Then we got a bit freaked out. *Why is it that all it takes is one evil person to ruin everything?*

Well, one thing was for sure—Dad's answer really helped Mom warm up to the idea of me going to Seattle, because she said suddenly, "Okay, I'll let Claire go."

"That's wonderful!" Darlene gushed.

"Really?" I nearly fell off my chair. "Are you serious?"

"Yes. But . . ."

I knew I wouldn't get off that easy. "But?"

"I know this may seem rude, but I would feel much better if Cassidy came, too."

Okay, yeah, that is rude. You can't just bring your kids along to hang out with other people when they haven't been invited. What is she thinking? I was about to die of embarrassment until I heard—

"Yes, great. I have no problem taking Cassidy too, especially if it means we get to have Claire with us." Darlene was much nicer about it than I expected her to be.

"Thank you! Thank you!" I couldn't help myself—I rushed over and gave Darlene a huge hug. "You're the best!"

"Hey, what are we, chopped liver?" my dad grumbled good-naturedly.

"You know I love you. Thank you." I hugged my parents. "Can I tell Cass, please? I can't wait to see her face."

"Sure, sure." My dad shooed me away. "We need to work out a few minor things with Darlene anyway."

That meant they needed to talk about how much it would cost. I wanted to be long gone when that conversation happened—no reason to feel guilty. "Okay!" I hollered as I skidded down the hall toward Cassidy's room and banged on the door. "Hey, I've got some news. Hurry up."

I could hear my parents and Mrs. Halloway chuckling behind me as Cass opened the door. "What's up?"

"Oh my gosh! You're never going to believe where we're going," I exclaimed as I pushed my older sister into her room and shut the door with my foot.

Cassidy laughed and swatted my hands away. "What do you mean? Are they planning a vacation or something?"

"Something like that."

Cass put her hands on her hips. "Okay, spill."

It came out in one big gush. "Oh my gosh! You know Darlene? Well, she came here to invite me to go to Seattle with her. Can you believe it? I'm totally dying here. Mom got overprotective and demanded that you come too—which I was seriously mortified about—but it doesn't matter because Darlene said yes! You get to come too, to Washington, for the whole summer! How cool is that?"

After my monologue, I was so busy catching my breath that it took me a moment to realize Cassidy wasn't jumping around the room like I thought she'd be. In fact, she looked downright upset about it.

"Hey, are you okay? What's wrong?"

"Do I have to go?" That was the last thing I expected to hear come from her lips.

"Are you kidding? You mean, 'Do I really get to go,' right?"

"No." Cassidy shook her head. "Do I have to go? Like, will Mom let you go without me?"

"There is something seriously wrong with my ears. I know you're not sounding disturbed by this amazing news. I know it." *Sheesh. What is this world coming to?* "And yes, to answer your question, I think Mom would totally freak out if you didn't come too. It was hard enough for her to let me go as it is." *No thanks to your antics with Blake.*

"Can you keep a secret?" Cassidy asked quietly.

No. I'm the worst at keeping secrets. Everyone knows that. "Um, sure. What is it?"

She frowned and looked nervously around the cluttered room as though she was checking to see if we were alone. With a gulp, she leaned forward and whispered, "Promise me you won't tell anyone, okay? Promise?"

Only people I can absolutely trust. "Promise."

Cass's eyes were huge. "I'm seeing someone."

Huh? "That's your secret? You're seeing someone?"

She looked perturbed. "Well, yeah. That's a big secret!"

"That you're seeing someone?" I snorted and plopped on her bed. "You're talking about Ethan, right?"

Cassidy's jaw dropped. "How in the—? Where did you—?"

"Chloe told me like a year ago."

"No way."

"Yeah. She told a lot of people. That's way old news."

"What? Did she tell Mom and Dad?"

"Um . . . no." I threw a crumpled T-shirt at her. "Chloe's not stupid. But I wouldn't be surprised if they already know anyway."

"Are you kidding me?" Cassidy threw herself on the bed next to me, obviously dejected. "Mom and Dad would have total seizures, and you know it."

She's probably right. "Come on, they're not that bad."

"Not that bad?" Cassidy flipped around and faced me. "Not that bad? You of all people should know what it's been like living through their 'grounding for life' episode." She fell back on the bed again. "Never mind that Ethan is only one of the nicest guys ever. And so different from Blake Winter, it's a joke. Mom and Dad don't trust me to make my own judgments when it comes to guys. I'm eighteen. Really, you'd think they'd lighten up!"

"Cass, it looks like they are," I pointed out. "If this vacation is anything to go by, they trust you a lot."

"Yeah, some trust—banning me from the one guy I have ever really loved for a whole summer."

"A guy they technically don't know exists." *Good grief. Maybe I don't want Cassidy to go if she's going to be a major mess.* "Think of it this way, Cass. If you manage to bring me back in one piece and prove to them that you're responsible, you could probably very easily include Ethan in the picture once you got home."

Cassidy sat up. The imaginary light bulb above her head flickered and then lit up. "I think you're right." She jumped off the bed and walked over to her window. "So, if I go for like a few weeks this summer, by the time I get back everything will be a whole lot better. I mean, they have to trust me, right?" She spun around with a huge smile on her face. "It's brilliant! Like totally mad-scientist perfect. If Mom and Dad trust me enough to babysit you all the way in Washington, then they'll have to trust me with everything else. Hee hee hee!"

Now she was dancing around the room.

"Come on!" She giggled. "We've only got what, three weeks until summer break? We've got to figure out what to pack!"

{♥}

Needless to say, I left my older sister much happier than when I'd gone into her room thirty minutes earlier. We planned everything, down to our party clothes, just in case we were lucky enough to go out somewhere. All in all, I was pretty pleased with the idea of going with Cass. She was a lot of fun if you knew her. Some people only saw her quiet side—the person she'd been ever since the Blake incident—but for a few minutes there, I got a glimpse of the old Cass, the Cass that probably only Ethan saw these days.

Hmm . . . maybe this trip will be better all around for a lot of reasons.

I softly closed my door and took a minute to just look around my bedroom. I'd turned sixteen earlier in the year, and I was now almost sixteen and a half. It was the perfect age—in the pre-Blake days—because it would have been the time when I could go on my first date. But because of Blake, Dad had threatened to make us wait until we were thirty. Okay, to be fair, I'm sure he would've relented and let me go on a date now if a guy actually asked me.

Yep. That was my sorry state of life. Sixteen, never been on a date, never been kissed, never held hands with a guy, never— well, never *anything*. Totally pathetic, right? I blame it mostly on my randomly weird parents—and the fact that after Chloe and Cassidy were born, there wasn't much magic left in the beauty wand for me.

Don't get me wrong. I'm pretty enough—just not knockout

gorgeous pretty. Take my sisters, for instance. Chloe is a stunning redhead with long, perfectly placed ringlets, who's practically engaged to the hottest guy in Farmington, New Mexico. And Cassidy has the same exact ringlets, just with bright blonde hair and a reputation for being either a massive wild-child flirt—thanks to Blake—or a soft-spoken mouse—again, thanks to Blake.

Anyway, how can you compete against a blonde and a redhead? Especially when I'm not sure what color my completely straight hair is. Sometimes people tell me it looks dirty blonde, and sometimes I've been told it looks brownish.

Fine. So there you have it. Me, Claire, the baby in a family of three girls whose total existence has revolved around the actions—and their consequences—of her older sisters.

With a sigh, I walked around my room almost as though I was seeing it for the first time. The feeling was pretty surreal, as if it knew I was about to leave and have an amazing adventure. *Washington!* Just thinking about it made me giggle again. I ran over to my desk, plunked down in the seat, and pulled down the book above me before my brain had even processed what I was doing.

Twilight was the most perfect book in the whole world, and subsequently, my favorite in the series. Carefully, I opened up the well-used paperback and allowed the pages to float down in a happy fan. I could feel the gentle breeze the papers made against my arm before they nestled down again. Almost by instinct, I thumbed through a couple of worn pages and found my favorite passage. It was, hands down, the most romantic paragraph ever written. I sighed as I read the words of Edward Cullen when he tells Bella that she is the most important thing to him now, and how the thought of hurting her has tortured him.

Then I quickly flipped a couple of pages until I came to the most poignant of all things ever said by Edward. I vividly remembered shaking when I first read his description of his desperate battle within himself to not kill Bella. All he wanted was to get her alone, but the thought of what killing her would do to his family kept him from it. Little did I know until that moment how much danger she'd been in! Edward wanted to kill her and had thought of ways to do it.

Bella Swan. The most amazing heroine ever written. I mean, what other female character had been so easily relatable, or so perfectly complex and lifelike? There couldn't be another heroine more wonderful than Bella—I was sure of it.

So there it was. My deep, dark secret, the reason behind my fascination with Washington. I was in love with Edward Cullen. And Edward lived in Washington. Plain and simple. According to Stephenie Meyer, Washington has the most rainfall of any state. And as everyone knows, vampires have to live in cloudy places.

Since the Twilight series, I had become rather addicted to and obsessed with all things pertaining to the world of Edward Cullen and Bella Swan. There was so much to learn. The funny thing was, every time I read one of the books, I found something new—something I'd missed before.

And then it hit me.

I'm going to Washington.

I'm really, really, really going.

Honestly, can life get any better than this?

Praise for *Northanger Alibi,* the next book in
The Jane Austen Diaries

"Stephenie Meyer meets Jane Austen in this humorous, romantic tale of a girl on a mission to find her very own Edward Cullen. I didn't want it to end!"

—Mandy Hubbard, author of *Prada & Prejudice*

"*Northanger Alibi* reminds us in comical, relatable ways that mythical creatures aren't always what they're cracked up to be, and that real boys can be even better."

—Eve'sFanGarden.com

"*Northanger Alibi* will have you laughing out loud at Claire's observations and dramatic responses. In a world where every teen girl is looking for her 'Edward' . . . , Claire's coming-of-age story is both timely and refreshing."

—Amanda Washington, author of *Rescuing Liberty*

"Absolutely wonderful and addictive."

—Brynna Curry, author of *Earth Enchanted*

"I fell in love with Claire and Tony the same way I fell in love with Edward and Bella in *Twilight. Northanger Alibi* has all the ingredients of a great love story."

—Greta Gunselman, killerromance.com

"*Northanger Alibi* is fun, exciting, and suspenseful. . . . James has hit the nail on the head with this one!"

—Keyth A. Pankau

"*Northanger Alibi* was a breath of fresh air. . . . The book, above all, has such a captivating love triangle, I couldn't put it down."

—Kari

STAY IN TOUCH WITH JENNI JAMES

****

Visit authorjennijames.com
to learn more about Jenni,
read interviews and reviews,
and get all the details on upcoming titles.

****

Become a fan on **facebook**
Author Jenni James
The Jane Austen Diaries

Follow me on **twitter** Jenni_james

Send me an [email] jenni@authorjennijames.com